for WITCHES OF EAST END:

"Centuries after the practice of magic was forbidden, Freya, Ingrid, and their mom struggle to restrain their witchy ways as chaos builds in their Long Island town. A bubbling cauldron of mystery and romance, the novel shares the fanciful plotting of Blue Bloods, the author's teen vampire series . . . [B]reezy fun." —*People*

"A magical and romantic page-turner . . . *Witches of East End* is certain to attract new adult readers . . . The pacing is masterful, and while the witchcraft is entertaining, it's ultimately a love triangle that makes the story compelling. De la Cruz has created a family of empathetic women who are both magically gifted and humanly flawed." —*The Washington Post*

"For anyone who was frustrated watching Samantha suppress her magic on *Bewitched*, Ms. de la Cruz brings some satisfaction. In her first novel for adults, the author . . . lets her repressed sorceresses rip." —*The New York Times*

"What happens when a family of Long Island witches is forbidden to practice magic? This tale of powerful women, from the author of the addictive Blue Bloods series, mixes mystery, a battle of good versus evil and a dash of Norse mythology into a page-turning parable of inner strength." —*Self*

"*Witches of East End* has all the ingredients you'd expect from one of Melissa's bestselling YA novels—intrigue, mystery and plenty of romance. But with the novel falling under the 'adult' categorization, Melissa's able to make her love scenes even more . . . magical." —MTV.com

GOLDEN

HEART *of* DREAD

BOOK THREE

MELISSA DE LA CRUZ
MICHAEL JOHNSTON

speak

SPEAK
An imprint of Penguin Random House LLC
375 Hudson Street
New York, NY 10014

First published in the United States of America by G. P. Putnam's Sons,
an imprint of Penguin Random House LLC, 2016
Published by Speak, an imprint of Penguin Random House LLC, 2017

THE LIBRARY OF CONGRESS HAS CATALOGED
THE G. P. PUTNAM'S SONS EDITION AS FOLLOWS:
Names: De la Cruz, Melissa, 1971– author.
Johnston, Michael (Michael Anthony), 1973– illustrator.
Title: Golden / Melissa de la Cruz, Michael Johnston.
Description: New York : G. P. Putnam's Sons, [2016] | Series: Heart of dread ; 3
Summary: Desperate to escape the dangers of the ruins of New Kandy, Nat and Wes
must put their love to the ultimate test by chancing even more perilous surroundings
in hopes of seeing their world reborn by saving the source of magic.
Identifiers: LCCN 2015049226 | ISBN 9780399257568 (hardback)
Subjects: | CYAC: Magic—Fiction. | Voyages and travels—Fiction. | Survival—
Fiction. | Love—Fiction. | Environmental degradation—Fiction. | Science fiction. |
BISAC: JUVENILE FICTION / Action & Adventure / Survival Stories. | JUVENILE
FICTION / Fantasy & Magic. | JUVENILE FICTION / Love & Romance.
Classification: LCC PZ7.D36967 Go 2016 | DDC [E]—dc23
LC record available at http://lccn.loc.gov/2015049226

Speak ISBN 9780425288306

Printed in the United States of America

1 3 5 7 9 10 8 6 4 2

For Mattie, always

GOLDEN

HEART *of* DREAD

BOOK THREE

He laughed and smote with the laughter and thrust up over his
    head,
And smote the venom asunder, and clave the heart of Dread;
Then he leapt from the pit and the grave, and the rushing river
    of blood,
And fulfilled with the joy of the War-God on the face of earth
    he stood
With red sword high uplifted, with wrathful glittering eyes;
And he laughed at the heavens above him for he saw the sun arise,
And Sigurd gleamed on the desert, and shone in the new-born
    light,
And the wind in his raiment wavered, and all the world was bright.
But there was the ancient Fafnir, and the Face of Terror lay
On the huddled folds of the Serpent, that were black and
    ashen-grey
In the desert lit by the sun; and those twain looked each on each,
And forth from the Face of Terror went a sound of dreadful
    speech:
"Child, child, who art thou that hast smitten? bright child, of
    whence is thy birth?"
"I am called the Wild-thing Glorious, and alone I wend on the
    earth."
    —WILLIAM MORRIS, *THE STORY OF SIGURD THE VOLSUNG*

THE DARK ROAD AHEAD

THE QUEEN LOOKED INTO AVALON'S Mirror and the mists parted to show her what she needed to see: the future as only she could shape it, the various roads ahead, the consequences of every decision.

She saw great armies in battle, shining cities laid to ruin, smoking and destroyed. Blood spilled on a great tundra of white. Bodies piled in stacks, burning.

The whole world on fire, hope lost, civilization a memory.

Every path, every possibility, led to devastation, to the end of everything.

The end of the world.

Every path, save for one.

The only way forward to a new beginning led to a golden ring inside a gray tower.

But if she chose that path, that future, everyone she loved would die.

No one would survive.

Not even her.

She studied the mirror at length and stepped away, closing her eyes. Things were what they were. Avalon could not save the future from itself.

Only one person could do that, she knew.

And in that moment, everything was decided.

PART THE FIRST

BATTLE AND PORTAL

The supreme art of war is to subdue the enemy
without fighting.

—SUN TZU

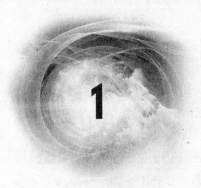

1

THE RUINS OF THE WHITE TEMPLE burned in the hazy distance, and from high above in the clouds, Nat could see the unholy city of New Kandy covered in a blanket of smoke, its tall towers now mere black skeletons.

The city was on fire.

Death was in the air, all around her. Nat could feel the grim grip of fate cutting deep into her bones. She knew it by the stench of the ash, the burning cinders in her eyes.

Ruination had come for them, for all of them.

Then the buildings' silhouette seemed to sway, as the vision wavered, flickering in and out of sight. Nat blinked her eyes and gritted her teeth, forcing the connection to return. For months she had used her drakon's powerful gaze to scan the horizon for enemies, to prepare for any hidden ambush, to notice changes in the battlefield that no mortal eye could hope to observe. That was the nature of her duty, the right of her destiny.

Or so it had been.

But now the thread between them was fraying fast, as a new bond was being forged between drakon and rydder. Helplessly sidelined, Nat found herself not where she should be—high above the clouds with her mount—but rather, sitting on the deck of a ferryboat, watching as her one true calling was stolen from her.

Because an imposter rode atop Drakon Mainas.

An imposter, and a murderer. A threat not just to Nat, but to the entire world, and any hope for its future.

Not to mention, a danger to the drakon itself.

Eliza.

She was to blame. The Lady Algeana, formerly known as Eliza Wesson, the child who had been stolen from her home by the people of Vallonis in order to save their world. But Eliza was the *wrong* child and she had grown up to become no one's savior.

Quite the opposite. She had taken what was not hers to take, and now everything lay in ruins as the result.

Nat could feel Eliza's heels digging into Mainas's hide, urging the creature to fly faster and higher away from the battle, fleeing from its true mistress. Nat fought back, desperately attempting to regain command of her drakon.

Mainas! Stay!

Do not leave me!

You're making a mistake!

You don't know what you're doing!

Nat felt a rage burn in her core as hot as the flame that swirled around the drakon's heart—and for a moment Eliza's hold slipped and the drakon reared, frantically attempting to buck her off her seat, lashing with its head and tail, shrieking with anger and pain.

But only for a moment.

Nat was too far away, and Eliza too strong, and every thunderous beat of wings and passing second widened the gap between them.

I am your mistress now. Eliza's calm voice cut through the smoke and fire. *You are mine to command.*

Nat could barely sense her drakon anymore, had to strain to hear the sound of the wind rushing beneath its wings, to feel the cold air around its scales. The thread between them was tearing, like fibers quickly spinning apart, unraveling what had been fiercely knitted together.

She held on as hard as she could to the drakonsight, gazing down upon a dark, burning landscape, at the remnants of a broken city, where at its edges, a battalion of tanks rolled across the blistered earth like ants converging on a hill.

Then it was gone. *No . . . not yet . . .* She had to hold on to her drakon. *Drakon Mainas!* she called again. *To me!*

Nat followed the slender line that led back to the mind of the monstrous green-eyed and black-scaled creature that was her own twin soul. She burrowed into its thoughts, screaming for it to hear her, to recognize her as its avatar.

We are one and the same, drakon and rydder! I am Anastasia Dekesthalias. The Resurrection of the Flame. The girl on your back is an imposter. You have been deceived!

Return to me! Mainas!

There was no response—only the dull weight of loss.

And then, abruptly, it was over.

The connection between Nat and her drakon snapped, and her vision disappeared into complete darkness. Eliza had finally succeeded in cutting the cord.

Nat lost her drakonsight. She no longer felt the pounding of the creature's heart, the strain of its muscles; its fury was no longer hers to command and unleash. The drakon was gone and Nat was alone.

She had lost her mount once before, had willingly sent it deep into the ground, to heal after a fierce firefight during her guardianship of Vallonis. But this was different. Something elemental was now broken and torn inside her—as if a piece of her very being had been taken away, and she was blinded, rendered deaf and mute. Senseless.

Drakon Mainas!

She screamed, even though she knew he couldn't hear her.

A moment later, Nat opened her eyes to the world around her. Everything looked fuzzy and gray, now that she had lost the keen eyesight of her drakon.

Reality was not something she wanted to come back to. Not yet. It was too hard and too cold and too painful. She had lost too much.

Where am I?

Snow was falling. That was one clue. She could smell it, even taste it. It was in her hair, on her filthy clothes, mixing with the ashes from the battle. She heard the tanks rolling through the streets from the sound of the rattling treads.

Beyond that, she could pick out the slightly higher pitch of the drones buzzing in the air above them. Like flies gathering around her location as they would around a dead body. Which was what Nat herself would soon be, if she stayed here where they could find her.

And where is that again?

The deck of a ferryboat.

Nat's eyes snapped into focus, and she found herself staring up at the stricken faces of her small, tired crew. Shakes crouched next to her while the smallmen, Brendon and Roark, held on to each other. Liannan's head remained bowed, her golden-blond hair falling across her face. Farouk stood frightened and grief stricken, his hands clenched at his sides.

And something else. *Someone else. A dead body.*

She looked down at the boy in her arms. Ryan Wesson lay motionless, blood crusting on his cheek, his face as frozen and gray as the floor beneath him.

It all came rushing back to her—the battle with Eliza, Wes using his newfound powers to dispel his sister's illusions. Victory and escape were in their grasp, until Eliza suddenly reappeared on Drakon Mainas's back while Wes had collapsed on the deck. Shakes had tried to jump-start his heart by pounding on his chest, but nothing had worked.

"Wes!" Nat cried, her tears making tracks through the dirt on her face. It seemed unreal, this moment. His lifeless face. The weight of his still body.

This couldn't be happening. *Just a moment ago, we were kissing—how can this be?* Now his lips were blue and his eyes were closed. He had saved them from Eliza, but at what cost?

Magic had consequences to its use. He couldn't wield its power without hurting himself, and no one could have imagined the toll it would take on him.

I didn't think it would do this. He couldn't have known, either.

Not that it would have made any difference to Wes, she knew. Nat stroked his cheek. He would have fought for her to the death, no matter what. But he didn't have to. She didn't want him to.

He didn't have to die.

He can't.

"Stay," she said, telling him the same thing she had said to her drakon not too long ago. "Don't leave me." She put a hand on his chest, willing whatever power she had left to flow into him, to keep him alive even just a moment longer.

Nothing happened. There was no spark of life in his pale face.

It was useless. She was useless.

"Nat, he's gone, and we need to move—they've spotted us," said Shakes gently, with a hand on her shoulder. "Roark— help me cast off the lines; Brendon, to the wheel; Farouk, see if you can get that engine running."

The boys exchanged uneasy glances as they swiftly carried out Shakes's orders.

Liannan caught Shakes's pleading look and moved quickly toward Nat. "Hey," she said softly. "There's nothing you can do for him anymore. And we need your help if we're going to get out of here alive."

Nat said nothing. Ashes in her mouth. Numb. Spent.

"Wes would want that, Nat. Don't make his sacrifice mean-ingless. He needs you to be strong. He wants you to live."

Nat ignored her. She ignored them all. They'd all given up on Wes, but she wasn't going to. He couldn't be dead; he couldn't leave her, not now. Not so soon after they'd found each other again.

She pressed harder against his chest, willing his heart to beat. Willing him to make his way back to her side.

She could live without drakonsight, without drakonlimb, without drakonwing. But she could not live if Wes did not.

The deck vibrated underneath her as the boat's engines sputtered to life—and then died just as quickly. Shakes cursed. "What the ice is going on back there?"

"Pipes are frozen solid," yelled Farouk from below. "And we can't get a fire started in the coal bin!" The ship had been retrofitted with a steam engine when its owners hadn't been able to fix its electric one.

"Nat, come on," cried Liannan, running toward the stern of the ferry. "Help me conjure a flame!"

Nat was made of drakonfire, but she remained still. She was sure that without her drakon, there was no fire left in her. She was unable to move, unable to breathe, as Wes's heart remained silent underneath her palm.

His heart had stopped and now hers was shattered.

She was no use to anyone. She couldn't keep him alive—she had no drakon, no fire, no power of her own. She was nothing; she was nobody.

Dimly, she heard the RSA forces swarming around the

burning city, recapturing the marked who were once prisoners in the White Temple, the very people Wes and his crew had just set free. Rounding them up one by one.

It was all for nothing.

A gunshot cracked in the distance, and Nat jumped. She turned to see—and from afar, she saw a body fall to the ground with a hard thump.

No. They weren't rounding up the prisoners.

They were executing them.

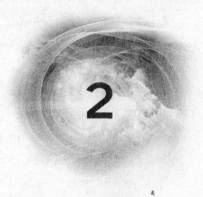

2

AM I DEAD?

Why can't I move? What's happening? What's wrong with me?

It took a while for Wes to figure out he had collapsed. Part of him was confused, because for a moment he was still standing, and he wondered if it was because kissing Nat was too much like a dream.

A beautiful, perfect dream.

To Wes, it wasn't quite real, as if he were unable to accept that they were together now, after everything they'd endured to get here.

They'd been kissing on the deck of the ferryboat. Nat's lips were open and soft against his. As he held her in his arms he marveled at her many improbabilities—so small and fierce, so much fury and strength in one person. He was looking forward to their life together, thinking about what they would do when they returned to New Vegas.

I don't deserve this. Her. Wes was so happy his head hurt.

Maybe that was the reason why everything looked pixelated and he felt as if he couldn't breathe.

Which he couldn't.

And all of a sudden, his knees gave way and he was falling.

Pull it together, man, it's just a kiss, he scolded himself. *And look what you've done, you've scared Nat.*

The last thing he remembered seeing was Nat's face, her eyes wide with shock, the ghostly pallor on her cheeks, her mouth open in surprise. He knew something had happened, and that it had something to do with him, even if he wasn't sure what.

"Wes," she called out. "Wes, no—"

I'm here, he tried to tell her.

She looked like she thought he was dying . . . and he wanted to say, *don't worry, I'm fine,* so that he could make her laugh again. Maybe kiss her again . . .

Then the convulsions began, and he tasted blood, it was coming out of his nose, his mouth, his eyes, he was bleeding . . . and everything went black . . . Now what . . . what was that? That *hurt*. A hard hit to this chest. Another one.

Ow.

Shakes. Pounding on him.

Ow.

Was that really necessary?

Tell him to stop, thought Wes. *I should tell him to stop.*

He'd just slipped, he was fine, he'd been kissing Nat and been overwhelmed by happiness, and maybe he'd lost his footing and he'd hit his head on the deck or something . . . no big deal because *he was fine* . . .

He was fine!

So why couldn't he move his hands? Why couldn't he

14

speak? And for that matter, why couldn't he open his eyes? And he was so cold . . . cold . . . and where was Nat? He couldn't feel her anymore . . . he couldn't feel anything . . . and he was cold and it was dark and *he couldn't breathe! He really couldn't breathe!*

What the freeze . . .

Oh man . . . Shakes was right to be alarmed . . . he *was* dying.

Godfreezeit . . . he was freezing dying . . . motherfreezer . . .

Nat . . . Nat . . . where are you . . .

Wes was in the dark for he didn't know how long. Then he heard a soft voice in his ear. It sounded familiar, although he couldn't place it. The voice tickled his consciousness, as soft as tendrils and as sweet as nectar, but imbued with a metallic cold.

You remember me, it said, replying to his thoughts as if it had heard him, and maybe it had.

Wes couldn't be certain, not of anything. Not now.

We met once before when you were a child. I visited you and your sister.

He stiffened.

Yes, I see, you remember now.

Wes would never forget that visit. He knew that voice. It was the same voice he'd heard the night he lost his twin.

Wes often dreamed of the night of the fire, the night Eliza had been stolen from her home. He dreamed of the meal his mother had cooked, a rare treat—a few cuts of meat and lumps of carrots and potatoes, cooked so long that it all had fallen into soft, warm strings in their bowls. They had eaten together as a family for once, as if they'd known it was the last time. He remembered his father flicking through the nets with his handheld before shooing them off to bed. The twins had shared a room, and in his dreams of that night Wes could still feel the heat from the flames that had engulfed the small chamber, licking the ceiling, curtains, and bedcovers. He remembered his terror and his confusion, and he remembered Eliza smiling.

He had never understood why.

He hadn't seen Eliza again until today. He had been searching for her his entire life, for only he understood the power that twisted inside her, and how easily it could be corrupted—as it was inside him as well.

The two of them were opposite sides of the same coin: Eliza, with her ability to absorb magic, and Wes, with his ability to block it. Magic had devoured her soul and turned it dark, but Wes was immune to its workings. He was a repellant, an antidote. He remained unaffected when she could not help but be devoured. He felt sorry for her, and she for him—unlike almost every other brother and sister they knew, who lived in a state of endless rivalry.

Not Eliza and Wes. Neither sibling wanted anything the other could do or have.

"I am the one you are looking for," the child Eliza had told the White Lady who stood in the middle of the fire that night, solemn and unafraid.

"So be it," the lady had said, and took Eliza by the hand.

I was wrong, the lady said now. Her voice echoed through Wes's frozen body and fallen mind.

I was mistaken. I was deceived.

Wes tried to open his eyes and see her for what she was, but he still could not move.

It does not matter. It is too late, Wes said to the lady. He thought the words so fiercely he was surprised he could not speak them.

She did not answer.

He tried again. *I am dying. It is too late.*

Again, she remained silent.

Wes felt like shouting now. *Too late for me. Too late for me and Nat. Too late,* he thought, his bitterness and disappointment as sharp as the happiness that had preceded it. *Leave me alone,* he told the lady in white. *Leave me to die in peace.*

The lady still did not reply.

Instead, another voice called to him from a great distance, a whisper that filled the cold darkness with unexpected heat, nourishing him like a warm broth, preventing him from falling deeper into the dark.

"Don't leave me!"

Was it just his imagination, or could he really sense a heart beating against his, soft hair falling on his face?

Nat. He wasn't dreaming this time. He was still alive, and Nat was cradling him in her arms.

Lovely Natasha Kestal. That's how he thought of her, even now. Even in this state. *My Nat.* Her warmth held back the darkness, keeping him on the edge of the light, the only thing that kept him upright.

I'm coming. He struggled to regain control of his senses, to follow her back toward the light. But the dark was so heavy, and he realized that Nat herself was struggling under the weight of it—and that if she continued trying, it would crush her. She couldn't keep his death away much longer, not without risking her own life. It was a miracle, and a testament to her strength, that she had held it off this long.

No, Nat. Stop. Wes wouldn't let her chance it. He couldn't let her. He wanted to tell her it was all right. She could let go.

Let go, Nat. He could die in her arms fulfilled.

She would live and that was all that mattered. She would grieve, but she would survive. Nat would keep living, and the thought gave him peace. Wes had died once before and he was not afraid. He was tired. He wanted to rest, to remain in the darkness and fade.

"Stay," said Nat again.

I can't.

Her warmth was fading and her strength would not keep the cold and dark out much longer without hurting her.

"Don't leave me." There were tears in her voice now, and it killed him.

But I have to.

She would only hurt herself trying to save him. It was better this way.

And so he did what she could not; he let go of her and fell—plunging deep into the darkness. He felt himself sinking away, deeper and deeper into shadow and cold. Nat's voice grew distant, her sobs quiet. A great nothingness on all sides, from all directions, enveloped him.

He felt his mind grow still, until he himself was like the silence . . .

But as he fell back through the darkness, he heard the sudden sound of a tank rumbling loudly, as if coming from the bottom of the ocean. The louder it grew, the more noise it seemed to bring with it—his friends screaming, Shakes yelling, Liannan giving orders.

Now he could almost feel Nat's arms tense around him.

One last attempt. The world would not give up on him so easily.

So he did what he had to—he struggled to force them all away. Every friend, every memory, every desire. Every thread was a threat. Every connection that bound them together was a wick to another stick of dynamite. He would not drag his friends down into the shadow worlds with him. Would not let them drown, when they had to fight.

It's not safe. Not even now. You have to let go—all of you.

He pushed them away until they were fading, fading, and the darkness welcomed him once again into its infinite embrace—greedy and voracious—as if to make up for lost time. He fell faster and deeper this time, and he scrambled for footing, but there was nothing but air. He felt his heart slow.

There.

Once again, it was hard to breathe.

Now.

Everything felt cold again. His fingers were numb, his legs frozen. *I'm going to have to find a better line of work when this is all over.* He wished he could laugh at his own joke, but the cold held his lips closed.

He couldn't hear Shakes anymore, couldn't feel Nat's heartbeat against his, and one by one Wes let go of everything—his memories, his thoughts—until he didn't know where he was, or who he was anymore, or even the name of the girl he loved more than life.

He no longer knew or cared.

It was over, and if he could, he would have mourned what he had never had.

3

"WELL, ISN'T THAT A PRETTY SIGHT," a voice drawled. "Not."

Avo Hubik, the slaver who was once again drafted into the military high command, was wearing a foolish, triumphant grin on his face as he preened from the top of the hulking white tank on the shore across from their boat.

The cannon of his tank was aimed right at their hull.

Nat looked up, her face streaked with tears, as Wes remained still as death in her lap. He was gone. She knew she had to accept it, had to live with it. She also knew her friends had needed her, and she had failed them. She hadn't helped them escape, and she had to live with that, too. She was the reason Avo's cannon was pointed at them now.

The boat rocked slowly in place, stranded, caught. New Kandy, the city of the White Temple, burned in the distance, as tourists scattered and prisoners fled from the pursuit of the RSA's relentless automatic weaponry. Not that there was any point to fleeing, Nat knew. The rat-a-tat-tats echoed through the streets, and even the water rippled from the explosions.

"I wouldn't do that if I were you," Avo said to Shakes, who'd reached for his gun. "I could blast you all to hell from where I'm standing. So let's behave. You can make this much more pleasant for yourselves. Come out with your hands up. Throw down your weapons. No funny business, now."

Shakes reluctantly put his gun down. Roark and Brendon did the same. Farouk and Liannan came out from the back, their arms raised.

This crew knew better than to run.

Nat simply watched, her grief and her exhaustion rendering her mute.

"That's it, that's it," said Avo, waving his pistol. "ON YOUR KNEES!"

One by one they went down, forming a circle around Nat and Wes. She appreciated the gesture, their friends protecting them to the last. Hands behind their heads, they were defiant even in defeat. Liannan's violet eyes were glittering in anger, but she was too weakened by her imprisonment in the White Temple to be able to act. Brendon and Roark stared straight ahead, unwilling to show fear. Even Farouk was silent for once, instead of anxiously jabbering. Shakes held his head high and proud, his jaw clenched. *Take your best shot.* That was the message. They might as well have been shouting it at the top of their lungs.

I should do something, Nat thought dully, but she had no strength left to call up whatever fire was left inside her. Her drakon was stolen. Wes was dead. There was nothing left. Soon, they would all be dead.

So she sat motionless. Watching as if it were happening to people she didn't know, didn't love.

Avo holstered his gun and jumped nimbly from the top of his tank to the deck of their boat. The former slaver looked the same as the last time they'd seen him, his hair dyed as snowy white as the frozen landscape. He walked casually toward the kneeling prisoners, keeping his gun cocked. He stopped and surveyed the group.

No one looked back at him.

"Like a message in a bottle you all came back to me. I'm touched, really," he said, with a smirk on his face and a hand dramatically fluttering on his heart. "Right here." He removed a flask from his jacket and took a loud gulp, the rancid stink of iceshine filling the air. "Regular cast of circus freaks, aren't you."

"What up, tool," he said, as he kicked Shakes with his boot.

Shakes spat at him but missed.

Avo shook his head, bemused. "Tsk, tsk, tsk. And I remember you," he said, turning to Liannan.

She glared.

"You're the dirtiest-looking sylph I've ever seen. What's the matter? Did they run you through the killing floor? Get your pretty hair mucked up?" Avo grabbed her by her hair and yanked her head back, displaying her white throat.

"Don't freezing touch her, you icehole," growled Shakes.

In answer, Avo let go of her and slowly raised his hand,

making the shape of a gun. He pointed it at Liannan's head before blowing mock smoke across its tip, replacing the flask in his jacket. "Too bad I missed the killing floor. It would have been fun hunting you down, watching you run—"

Shakes moved to strike, but Avo twisted and fired first.

Liannan screamed as Shakes went down, clutching his leg, which was bleeding from the calf.

"Touchy, touchy." Avo laughed, using his revolver to slam Liannan in the back so that she fell forward with a cry as she hit the deck.

Shakes crawled to help, but Avo kicked him away easily as he made his way into the inner circle of the group, where Nat sat holding Wes.

The slaver loomed over Nat. "Get up," he ordered.

She ignored him.

"Are you deaf, girl? I said get up!"

Reluctantly, Nat laid Wes gently on the deck and stood to face him. Indeed, Avo Hubik was as sleek and handsome as he had been the last time they'd met on the black waters, when he'd taken the crew captive. Ageless as a vampire, unmarked by war or grime, and the venom in his voice was the same.

"I think it's high time I added that lovely skull of yours to my collection," Avo said, pointing to the glistening white tank idling behind him. Nat couldn't help but see what he meant. Three shriveled heads were mounted on its grill, their mouths open in a silent scream.

Nat shuddered.

Avo grinned. "Plenty of room for more." He looked down at the sight of Wes's body. "Haven't we been here before? But this time, he should stay dead," Avo said, giving Wes a swift kick in the head.

Nat stepped between them. "Go near him again and you'll regret it forever."

"As if." Avo laughed, wagging his finger, clearly savoring the moment.

Nat waited for him to strike her, but he did not. Instead, he turned to the group. "I told you back then that Wesson would only lead you to your deaths. And look. I'm a freezin' prophet. Any last words?"

"None for you, icehole," Shakes replied with his usual glibness. "Although a last meal would have been welcome."

"Now you're talking. Avo would make a lovely steak, don't you think? With a side of béarnaise," added Roark.

"Accompanied by a glass of Upper Pangaea's finest," said Brendon. "I always find that goes well with filet of icehole."

"Filet of heat bag," corrected Roark. "Chewier."

"Right!" Brendon laughed.

"SHUT UP," Avo snapped, moving his gun from one insolent smallman to the next, irritated by their camaraderie—and that Wes's crew was acting as if they were at a dinner party rather than an execution.

He whistled for two of his soldiers to join him on the deck.

There was an uneasy silence from Wes's team as Avo's men came forward, rifles slung across their shoulders, and ugly, blood-crusted knives tucked into their belts.

"I see you recognize my new recruits," Avo drawled. "From what I heard things didn't end too well between you all. Pity, but then revenge is a powerful motivator. It can make us do things we might normally find . . . what is the word? Abhorrent? I never made it to upper school, so someone tell me."

The Slaine brothers, Daran and Zedric, exchanged nasty smiles. "Abhorrent sounds about right," said Daran, the older and more dangerous one. The two of them had been part of Wes's crew until Daran attacked Nat when he discovered she was marked. In retaliation, Nat's drakon had thrown him into the black ocean and the crew had left him for dead. The next evening his brother, Zedric, stole away with Farouk and most of their supplies.

From the look on their faces now, Nat could tell these were not bygones.

Avo patted his two new pets on the back, slinging an arm over each brother. He might as well have been holding robodogs on leashes. Snarling creatures designed for the kill.

"I'll let my boys take it from here to do their worst," Avo said, with another smirk. "I've got a date with the Lady Algeana." He scanned the skies. "Though if the witch thinks she's going to escape with that monster, she's barking mad."

For the first time since losing Wes, Nat felt something. A surge of anger. That this loser could speak like that of her drakon. She was incredulous and furious.

Then she felt something else. *Opportunity.* She drew herself up. "What's it to you? What do you want with the creature?" Nat asked. She tried to say it casually, but it was no use.

Avo only laughed. "Wouldn't you like to know." He motioned to the dead heads mounted on his tank's wheel casing, as if to remind her what lay in store.

As Nat stared at the skulls, she found she wasn't scared. It was too late for that. She had lost her heart twice in one day. Maybe she couldn't save Wes, but she wasn't going to let anything happen to her drakon.

And Avo is going to help me, whether he knows it or not.

Avo ordered his platoon to turn back to the city. "Radio the drones; we're going hunting."

Nat ignored his threat, her mind racing from what he'd told her. Avo was after her drakon, and Nat knew where Eliza had taken it. To the Gray Tower, to destroy it and the treasure it held—the spell that would fix their crumbling world.

Eliza meant to set the tower afire, to spread her darkness and her terror and her hate. So she could break and twist the world into something that matched her own broken and twisted experience.

But if Avo and his army were after Eliza and the drakon, it would slow her down, keep her from accomplishing her terrible mission.

The enemy of my enemy is my friend, Nat thought wryly, finding irony in the situation. Avo was helping their cause even as he promoted his own.

Good, thought Nat. Do that. Chase her down. Keep Eliza from the tower. Keep her from destroying what little hope they had left.

Just don't touch my drakon.

Before he died, Faix had left her with the two tokens, a small gray key and a golden charm. Nat remembered the words he had left her, too, as clearly as if he had spoken to her at this very moment.

Find the Archimedes Palimpsest. *Recast the binding spell. Light the flame. Make the world anew.* Faix believed in her, she thought, her eyes shining. She couldn't let him down, couldn't let his death mean nothing.

Not his death, and not Wes's.

But how can I fix the world, thought Nat, *when I can't even bring one lousy heart back to life?*

The skulls on the tank shook as it rumbled to life in front of her as Avo walked toward it.

The Slaine brothers sprung into action. "Get the chains on her. On both of them," ordered Daran, meaning Nat and Liannan. "What the freeze are you waiting for?"

Nat heard the sound of iron chains jangling as Liannan was restrained. Her own would be next. Iron to dampen the magic they held. Iron to keep them weak and bound.

Think, Nat. Do something. Make it matter.

Two choices lay before her—she could muster up the strength to fight, to make a stand and rally her crew to her side, or she could try to bring Wes back one more time.

It was one or the other. She didn't have enough power to do both. Fight them or heal him. She only had one chip to play, one last card to draw.

And there was only ever one choice for Nat.

COME BACK TO ME, she willed, as she placed both

hands on Wes's chest and sent the last of her fire into his soul. The white spark left her fingers just as the iron collar was clamped around her neck.

Come on, Wes. Wake up. Come on. Make your way back to me. You know the way. We've done it before and we can do it again.

4

A FIRE WAS BURNING INSIDE HIM.

No, no, please—

A spark lit him up from the inside, warm and forgiving.

Let me be—

A life force—*Nat's* life force.

That's her name—

Nat.

He remembered now.

And with that, he knew everything about her, all at once. The girl he had met in New Vegas at a blackjack table. The girl he had transported across the black ocean and into the Blue. The girl who rode the drakon. The girl he loved.

She loves me and she needs me.

Every ounce of Nat's strength and her love rushed into him, banishing the cold and the dark for good.

I cannot leave her like this. His heart thumped loudly in his chest, each beat stronger than the last. *I will not.*

And then suddenly, miraculously, his body obeyed.

Wes didn't know how or why—but he could feel the change coming. Weightlessness became weight. Breathlessness became breath. A thousand cold hands suddenly let go of him, pushing him back up to the surface of the immense darkness. Wes felt the air suck into his chest, and the fire spark back into his heart. He twitched a single finger. It tapped against the deck like a moth.

Good. I can move.

It was all Wes could do not to try to sit up immediately, but when he felt Nat move away, instinct told him to hold, to wait. *She's in danger.* His neck prickled with adrenaline. *Surrounded.* He could feel the tension all around her.

His senses told him they weren't out of the clear and he didn't have all his strength back yet. Feeling came back to his body slowly, working out from the center of his chest, out toward his toes, his fingertips.

His hearing sharpened. He recognized the heavy footsteps of his former comrade, accompanied by the smell of hair dye and two-credit snowshine, the kind of alcohol that got you drunk way too fast.

Avo Hubik. *What icy luck.*

Wes and Avo had fought on the same side of the war once, had been brothers in arms. Comrades. Soldiers. Heroes. They even had the same scar above their right eyebrow.

Then Avo had changed.

He began to take the jobs Wes had rejected. He trolled the black waters, doing the RSA's dirty work. He took slaves

31

to the flesh markets and to the White Temple. He'd been rewarded with his own military command, of course, and all the perks that came with it. Somewhere along the way, he'd lost the person he used to be. The soldier had turned slaver.

Meanwhile, Wes had survived on the margins of New Vegas, working his way down until he was hustling low-paying cons, playing coyote to those who wanted out of its borders. While Avo collected heat credits and kept his belly full of real meat and mead, Wes ate glop and swilled Nutri.

After Wes had left Nat at the Blue, he'd been forcibly re-drafted into the service. It had been the most miserable time of his life and he quickly abandoned his post when he and Nat had found each other again. Unlike Avo, Wes didn't have a tank or a command or a perk to his name, and that was fine with him.

More than fine. Wes twitched the fingers on his left hand into a fist. *Better.*

There was the loud clink of chains, which meant they had collared Nat. Liannan, too, most likely. RSA policy was to kill or subdue any marked or magic user first. He'd have to work fast. Wes strained to hear what else was going on—Avo was leaving—a stroke of luck. No. He'd called on more of his boys. Wes recognized the bickering voices but couldn't believe it at first.

Godfreezeit—the Slaine brothers. *Godfreezing freezeit*—back from the dead and with chips on their shoulders the size of Santonio. *Fate's freezing fist*—

It was all Wes's fault; he should never have taken them on his team. He'd done his best to train them, to try to mold them into good soldiers, men who followed orders and did the right thing. He'd tried to show them a way out of bitterness and hatred. But the brothers had never listened to him, never endeavored to be more than thugs.

Without his influence, they had been left to fend for themselves, to let their darker nature fester and take over what little humanity they had left. From the sound of it, Avo had turned them into monsters.

"Didn't think you would see us again, did you?" Daran was saying to Wes's crew.

Wes opened his eyes slightly.

Hello, Daran. Can't say it's a pleasure to see you again.

The impatient, angry boy they had traveled the toxic seas with had been transformed during his time in Avo's unit. Daran was no longer reckless and impulsive, but cruel and calculating, like his new commander. Wes could read it in the yellowing crisscrossing scars across his left cheek, his two missing fingers and his dead stare. He had nothing left to live for and nothing to fear.

Just another frozen, living dead.

Daran lazily spun his knives. "Let's see, where should we start? Maybe with these two? As an appetizer?" He laughed, an ugly bray, as he pointed to Brendon and Roark.

Wes glanced another familiar face.

Zedric. The brother.

The look in his eye was equally inhumane.

"Good one, bro," Zedric nodded, cleaning his bloodied knife on his pant leg. "Shall we?" he asked, setting his knife underneath Brendon's trembling chin.

"Nah, hold on."

Zedric twisted around angrily. "What?"

"Just cool it with the blade," Daran said. The brothers were only a year apart, but Daran had always treated his younger brother like a kid. "I've got something else in mind."

"Come on, man," Zedric asked. "Let's do 'em and be done with it."

Daran shook his head. "I said cool it."

Zedric shrugged. "Whatever."

Wes suspected that underneath the bravado, Zedric was nervous and scared. *He should be,* Wes thought; Zedric had seen Nat toss Daran across the deck without lifting a finger, had witnessed Liannan's power on the black ocean. There were images of Nat riding the drakon all over the nets.

They should all be scared of Nat.

She stood with her back to him now. He wished he could see her face, but he was glad he couldn't—one look at her and he would have been unable to keep himself still, not for even a moment longer.

Zedric reluctantly withdrew his knife, but not without cutting a thin red line on Brendon's neck, just because.

Brendon didn't squirm, didn't cry. Wes was proud of him.

"We need to do this slow—take our time, have some fun with it. Know what I'm saying?" Daran told his brother, his lips curving into a sick semblance of a grin.

"Wes should have let you drown," said Shakes, looking like

he wanted to draw a blade of his own. "Guess you caught that life preserver he tossed you, huh? Bobbed in the black ocean until you were picked up by an RSA patrol, is that it? Yeah, maybe next time he won't be so merciful."

Daran turned red. "SHUT UP!" And even though he'd told his brother to put away his knife, he pressed his own dagger against Shakes's cheek, drawing blood. It dripped in a line down to his jaw. "Is that what you call mercy? You guys left me for dead!"

"Well, not exactly," replied Shakes calmly, as the blood trickled down off his face. "If I recall things correctly, we didn't exactly leave you. We had no wind and no motor. We had no way to rescue you. And, if I'm correct, it was you who got yourself thrown overboard in the first place. You fired on Liannan and angered the drakon. Not too smart, but then you never were, were you?"

"I SAID SHUT UP!" Daran yelled, and hit Shakes on the head with the butt of his rifle, knocking him out cold.

Liannan's eyes welled with tears, but they didn't fall.

Farouk was less restrained and addressed the younger brother. "What do you think's the matter, Zed?" he asked. "Daran afraid of the truth?"

"Can't believe you went back to this sorry excuse for a crew, man," said Zedric, shaking his head. "Told you to stay with us. Now look where you ended up."

"I'd rather die a man than live a slave," said Farouk. "That's all you are. Avo's slaves."

"Oh, you're gonna die all right," muttered Daran, as Zedric raised his club.

"And I'll show you a man," Zedric growled, swinging as hard as he could.

But nimble Farouk ducked from the blow, and when Zedric missed again, Farouk laughed until Daran came to help, catching Farouk right in the face with a hard punch.

Farouk fell to the deck. Wes winced. *Two down and two chained.* Only Brendon and Roark left. He'd have to count on them for backup.

Wes kept still, waiting for the right moment to strike. Whatever he planned to do, he'd have to do it fast—once the element of surprise was gone, he'd be at a disadvantage. He slowly clenched his fists, one after the other now, testing his reflexes.

"Forget the midgets," he heard Daran say. "I want her."

Her.

He meant Nat.

Of course.

Wes kept his eyes closed and gritted his teeth. It took all of his willpower not to rise and hit him in the face. Daran had it in for Nat from the beginning. Wes had always known that he'd been obsessed with her for being marked, being different.

But that wasn't all. Daran also hated her for being beautiful and not returning his own attraction. Wes knew the type, the thugs in New Vegas who catcalled girls only to slash their faces when the girls didn't respond to their advances. Those who would destroy what they could not have.

Daran never had a chance with Nat, whether Wes was around or not, and knowing that only made him hate her even more.

"Time to stop playing around," Daran said. "Finish what we started back there on the water."

Wes raised his eyelids a little more to see what was happening, his heart beating painfully in his chest.

Daran now had Nat in a close embrace, his mouth against her ear.

Wes bristled.

"I heard the marked are good luck," Daran whispered. "Maybe I'll cut out your eyes and string them on a necklace." His hand cupped her chin, and turned her to face him. "What do you think? Or make a belt out of your hide? Carve a buckle from your bones?"

Nat remained silent as stone, gazing at him with contempt.

"But before I do, I think . . . I think I'd like a taste of what Wesson had," he leered.

Wes felt his strength returning as his fury grew.

Don't even think it.

"We'll share," said Zedric eagerly. "Both of them," he said, seeming to find courage in his brother's perversion. "Come," he said, pulling Liannan up by the hair and laughing. "Or should we make the little ones watch?"

I'll kill you both, with my own hands. Wes kept still, his eyes trained on the knife tucked inside Daran's waistband. *Closer, closer,* he thought. *Come closer.*

"Make them all watch," said Daran, his long pink tongue tracing a line from Nat's neck to her collarbone. "If only your boyfriend wasn't dead so he could see this," he said.

"He's not dead," Nat said bravely. "And when he wakes up you'll wish you were."

"Yeah, right." Daran laughed. With a swiftness powered by lust, he pushed Nat down to the deck, forcing her flat on her back, right next to Wes. He could hear her uneven breath as she tried not to panic.

Hold on, Nat, Wes thought. *Hold on. I'm here. Let him come closer. Just a little closer.*

Daran grinned down at Nat and motioned to Wes. "I'm going to enjoy making you mine next to his dead body."

"As if," Nat sneered, unafraid. She was baiting him, knowing Daran was easier to fight when he lost his temper. Wes knew it, too, but that didn't make it any easier to watch.

Daran kicked her in the stomach.

You'll pay for that, thought Wes.

Nat coughed, then laughed. "Coward."

"Witch, you'll see for yourself," Daran said. When he bent over her, covering her body with his, Nat screamed, her arms flailing around Daran's back.

Wes saw his chance and took it. He rolled up in a flash to grab the knife from Daran's waistband, but it wasn't there— *huh? What?* He looked up and saw Nat holding it in her hands as she plunged it deep into Daran's back.

Nice work, he thought, admiring her speed and ferocity as she quickly rolled away.

"Miss me, icehole?" Wes asked as he pounded Daran's head with his fists, sending him sprawling.

"What the freeze . . . ," gurgled Daran, blood pouring from his mouth. He turned around, his eyes wide. "You . . . I knew you were ice trash from the beginning." He pointed at the small white star that was shining above Wes's eyebrow, the one everyone had thought was just a scar, even Wes.

Wes knew better than that now, of course. It was his mark, the one that let the world know he was one of the children of the ice. Marked by magic. Just like Nat.

"Then we're even, 'cause Shakes was right," Wes huffed as he pressed his foot on Daran's back and removed the bloody knife, making Daran scream from the pain. "I should have let you drown."

Daran choked in a puddle of his own blood.

Wes bent to help Nat stand. "You're okay?" he asked.

She stared. "And you're not dead?"

He shook his head and shot her a cocky grin. "Who, me? And leave you?" he said huskily, all seriousness now.

They didn't say a word after that. *Later,* his eyes seemed to say, meeting hers. *Later,* her fingers seemed to agree, as they twisted around his. They heard nothing, saw no one else—

Until the sound of muffled screams interrupted them.

"Liannan!" Nat cried, pointing to the other side of the boat, where Zedric had disappeared with the sylph. In all the excitement during the attack on Daran, Wes had almost forgotten the other brother—and what he had threatened to do.

"Here!" yelled Roark, who was nearest to the struggling Liannan.

Wes tossed him the knife, and Roark jumped up and slashed at Zedric's arm, making an ugly gash. Liannan broke away from Zedric's grip, gasping, her robe torn.

"What the ice . . . holy freeze, you're supposed to be dead!" Zedric yelped when he saw Wes.

"Sorry to disappoint you." Wes shrugged.

"Don't worry, he will be," said Daran from his prone position on the floor, bleeding heavily, his face contorted into a vicious mask, holding up his automatic and pointing it at the reunited couple.

"Oh, for freeze's sake," said Wes, annoyed it wasn't over, but even before he'd cursed, he was already reaching for one of the guns his crew had laid down on the deck. He had it cocked and pointed at Daran's face when Nat stayed his hand. "Let me."

"But—you're still wearing the iron collar . . ."

She shook her head with a smile. "It doesn't matter now. I have you." Her iron chains broke, one by one, crashing to the floor.

"That's my girl," Wes said, grinning proudly. "Now go and smoke 'em."

5

NAT TURNED TO DARAN, HER GREEN-GOLD eyes glinting. "Any last words?"

"Ice you," Daran cursed as he hit the automatic, releasing a spray of bullets, but she waved them away as if they were pesky flies, and they disintegrated harmlessly into ashes. He kept firing until he was out of ammunition, his eyes full of panic as Nat bore down on him.

She leaned over him, her rage growing, wanting nothing more than to litter the deck with his bloody carcass. He had put his lips in her ear. He had panted and slobbered, warm and wet, on her skin. He had tried to take her by force and infect her with his hatred, his fear.

But if she killed him she would be just as wrong as he was. Just as twisted with revenge and hatred. She shook her head. She would spare his life, if only because she cared for hers.

As if Wes could read her mind, he reached into his pockets and removed a pair of standard military-issue handcuffs and locked them around Daran's wrists, chaining him to the rail.

She nodded to Wes, who cocked his head in approval.

"HELP! HELP! COME BACK! TURN AROUND!" Zedric yelled into his comm. "We're being attacked!" Screaming, Zedric viciously kicked at Roark—and his knife—and managed to skitter away before Nat could even raise a hand.

Brendon grabbed his gun from the floor and began to shoot after the fleeing target.

"GET HIM!" yelled Roark.

But Zedric was zigzagging away, and the bullets missed. He disappeared into the smoking, burning city, still yelling for Avo and his battalion to return.

Liannan went to work at Shakes's side, while Roark attended to Farouk. Before long, it seemed both would be back to consciousness. Wes had returned to life for them—all of them—just in time.

"How?" she asked, wondering at his brightly shining eyes, his worn but strikingly handsome face, his steadily beating heart. He was so incredibly alive, she almost couldn't believe it herself.

"You," he replied simply. "You did it."

"It worked?" she said, unbelieving. *He's a miracle. My miracle.*

"You bet it did," he smiled. "Like I said, I couldn't leave you."

"Never," she said.

"Never," he echoed.

"Swear it," she said.

He took her hands in his, pressed his forehead to hers. "I will never leave you. I give you my oath, because you are my oath. You are the one thing I would swear upon."

Their fingers laced together, and Nat felt the warmth flow between them, until she could no longer feel the edge of her own heart, the place where she left off and Wes began. *We are one thing again, as we were always meant to be.*

Nat stood on her tiptoes, and Wes bent forward, but before their lips could meet, an explosion rocked the boat.

Wes grabbed Nat by the arm, steadying the two of them against the rocking deck.

"Boss!" yelled Shakes. "We've got incoming!"

"Bazooka," Roark shouted back. "Zedric's got himself a motherfreezin' bazooka launcher."

Zedric fired again. Another missile flew, blowing a second hole in their boat.

Nat ducked. Wes dropped behind her. The deck splintered beneath their feet, and water began to spray up through the hull. So much for escape.

"We'll cut through the city," said Wes, pulling him and Nat back up. "Take over a tank and get it through the mountains to the other port. Find another boat there."

"Right on." Shakes nodded, his arm slung over Liannan's shoulders. "Come on, this way."

But before they could move, Zedric scrambled over the bow and flung himself back on the boat, bent on revenge. "How do you like this now, iceholes!"

He aimed his weapon right at Farouk and pulled the trigger. The bazooka recoiled as he fired. Time slowed as the muzzle exploded in fire—

And as Nat and Wes and the crew watched, half of Farouk's body disappeared in front of their eyes.

One minute his legs were there. The next, gone. Farouk's life with them.

"NO!" yelled Wes as the youngest member of his crew fell dead.

Wes tackled Zedric, bringing both them tumbling to the ground. Wes kicked the bazooka away, but Zedric managed to free himself.

It was Nat who blocked his escape, stepping directly into his path. Zedric launched a fist at her jaw but the blow never landed. It met the butt of Shakes's fist first. He caught Zedric's hand and twisted his wrist. Nat had never seen Shakes so angry.

"This is for Farouk," Shakes said, his voice hoarse and his eyes shining with tears. "And Liannan."

"Then give this to them," said Zedric with a smile, showing Shakes the wicked blade he held in his other hand. Shakes tried to pull away, but Zedric held on—and laughed as he carved an ugly wound in Shakes's side.

"Stop it!" Nat screamed.

Shakes shuddered and doubled over in pain, but before Zedric could strike again, Liannan was already there.

She raised her hands and a force stronger than wind picked up the knife and sent it flying.

Zedric fell to the floor, and before he could move, Wes had already restrained him and cuffed him to the rail next to his brother.

The rest of the crew stood in silence, breathing heavily after the fistfight, trying to get their bearings and solemnly taking in all that remained of Farouk. He was one of them. He was theirs to mourn, and theirs to bury.

And he was so young, Nat thought. *Too young.*

"Farouk," said Brendon, his face streaked with tears. "We can't leave him here with them."

Liannan tended to Shakes's wounds, chanting in some language Nat could not understand. Shakes ignored his own injuries, letting his own tears fall instead for the loss of Farouk and the end of one of their own.

"We have to," said Roark. "He would have been the first to say it. 'Get your freezing asses out of here,' he'd say." He smiled at the memory of their friend.

"He's right," Shakes said. "That's just what he'd tell us to do."

"Yeah, I know," Wes said. "It's just . . . ." His voice trailed off.

Nat nodded, even though she had no desire to leave Farouk, either. Just as she would not have left Wes. Not next to their enemies, next to his murderers, to freeze in the cold without a proper burial. But they had no choice but to do so.

Wes knelt next to Farouk's broken body and gently closed Farouk's eyelids. Liannan whispered a word of prayer and nodded to the others. Wes and Nat took the lead, Liannan followed, helping Shakes, and the remaining members of the team jumped off the boat and followed them into the burning city.

Even after everything she had seen, Nat was still stunned by the devastation wreaked by the RSA upon the temple city so quickly.

All around them was chaos.

There was no law and no mercy. Only violence for the sake of violence, and destruction for the sake of destruction. The few remaining drones and soldiers who hadn't peeled away with Avo's troop were firing on fleeing prisoners, herding them into corners and alleyways before executing them all.

The RSA hadn't returned to take back the White Temple; they had come to destroy it. To show the marked prisoners what happened when they attempted revolt, attempted escape. The whole city was a killing floor.

Wes took the lead and Nat covered the back, Liannan and Shakes trying to keep up with Shakes's bad leg, while Roark and Brendon yelled at any prisoner they could find to join them.

"Pick up the pace back there," Wes yelled. "Come on!"

"But we can't leave them here; we have to do something!" yelled Brendon, helping a young boy to his feet. The mark on the boy's chest was evident, even at a distance.

"Nat! Behind you!" Wes shouted as he took out a drone that fired on them, from where it hovered in the air above the next intersection. It exploded in front of them, sending flaming debris skittering their way.

Nat turned back to find a group of soldiers rushing at them from all sides.

She raised her hands and, with one swift gesture up, sent every weapon within sight flying to the sky, ripping them out from soldiers' hands, breaking fingers and tearing muscle.

This is for Farouk.

Cries echoed through the snowy air.

This is for Faix.

The strength of her attack lifted some of the men off their feet.

This is for Drakon Mainas.

A few clutched bloody hands, searching in the snow for lost fingers.

For the hole in Shakes's belly.

She was just getting started.

For the fear in Liannan's throat.

Leather ripped as knives flew from sheaths.

And for Wes.

The sound of crunching metal filled the air.

This, and everything, is for Wes.

It was a sick, awful, mechanical sound, but Nat thought it sounded wonderful. It was the sound of their weapons made useless by her power and her rage. She was the rydder after all, wasn't she? The girl who tamed the drakon.

Fear made the soldiers tremble. As their weapons sunk into the snow, bent and folded, they retreated, one step, then another, exchanging confused glances before they ran the other way.

"Follow me! Hurry," she said to another group of prisoners huddled in a corner.

"Over here," signaled Wes, leading the way, already across the street. His face was streaked with grime from the gunpowder all around.

"Wait, wait," said Liannan. Shakes was limping and leaning on her in order to walk. She slung an arm around his torso and propped him up.

"You'll be okay," Nat said to Shakes. *You have to be. We can't lose you, too.*

Shakes nodded. His leg and torso were bandaged with Liannan's white silk. The blood seeped through the fabric, but he tried not to look pained. He kept his head up.

"He'll make it," said Liannan, her face fierce with determination. "I've got him; let's go."

"I'm okay." Shakes was breathing heavily as he slumped against her.

They ran across the intersection, as the bombs continued to drop from the sky, and the screams of the dying echoed through the broken city, accompanied by the constant staccato of gunfire.

Nat hung back, making sure all the prisoners had crossed, looking over her shoulder in case anyone ran after them. This was her crew as much as Wes's. She would keep them safe. She had to.

Sure enough, the soldiers had regrouped, and now they were carrying broken pieces of glass and twisted pieces of steel as their weapons, ready to attack again. Nat turned to them, her eyes filled with fury. She was sick of fighting but she would fight to the last.

Don't these iceholes ever learn?

6

"WHERE'S NAT?" WES YELLED AS ROARK and Brendon crossed the intersection with a number of marked prisoners.

Roark shook his head while Brendon gaped at Wes. "We thought she was with you!"

Wes cursed and kept his eye out for her as he fired a few rounds at their attackers. But there was still no sign of Nat. Shakes and Liannan brought up the rear, and the whole group stumbled into the alleyway. "Where's Nat?" he demanded again.

This time, Wes didn't wait for an answer. Instead, he fought his way back to the open intersection.

There she was.

Nat was surrounded by soldiers on all sides. They were hurling anything they could find through the snowy air at her. She was ducking and weaving, pushing them away with only the force of her mind. A rock crashed upon her magic, shattering to pieces just as a second hunk of concrete hit the same invisible barrier. It bounced off, but a third was able to pierce through her shield, nearly striking her head. Another exploded in midair, the debris hitting everyone, the soldiers, Nat. *She's growing weaker,* Wes realized, agitated at the distance between them and trying to close in faster. A concrete block shattered in the place where she had been standing just a moment earlier.

"Nat!" he cried, pushing his way toward her, but he could barely see her from the back of the crowd. The soldiers pressed forward, forming a tighter circle around her, hurling cracked bricks and the broken fragments of signs, shards of glass, sections of steel beams, and fractured window frames.

"I've got this!" Nat cried, when she saw Wes shoving and kicking everyone who stood between them, slowly but surely coming her way.

"No chance," he shouted back at her. *Not on your life or mine.* He knew she wanted him to run. He knew she only wanted all of them to be safe. But Wes could never feel safe if she was in danger.

She was his heart, and it didn't beat without her.

A rock struck her in the face, and a second one hit her chest. More blood, more bruises. She staggered back, lost her footing. They lobbed a broken window at her, jagged glass hanging half out of the frame, and Wes pitched forward, putting his body between hers and the glass, absorbing the blow as it struck him. Nat closed her eyes, summoning her strength. In a flash of light, she propelled the pieces of wreckage hurtling back toward the soldiers, sending the men running, ducking for cover, leaving them alone for now.

She had bought them a brief reprieve.

"Motherfreezer," Wes said, groaning from the cuts on his back from the broken glass. The streets were eerily quiet.

"Are you okay?" asked Nat, helping him stand.

He winced. "I'll live. You?"

She nodded. She was all right. He exhaled in relief that he hadn't been too late.

"Where's the team?" she asked.

"Up ahead. I told Shakes to get out of the city and follow the trail in the mountains," he said, but even he knew it was a long shot. The RSA was sure to capture them first. Then he grimaced as a shooting pain erupted from the side of his head, and a voice whispered through the chaos.

Let me in. The lady in white. In his head. Again.

She visited him in his hour of death, and now she'd come back for him. He let her in once, and now he couldn't keep her out. For some reason, the thought filled him with a particular dread.

"Wes? What's wrong?" Nat looked worried.

"Nothing." Wes shook his head.

Foolish boy. Remain still, said the lady in white. The one who had stolen Eliza. The one who had spoken to him in the darkness. Was she the reason he was still alive now? But hadn't it been Nat who had brought him back from the deep dark? To whom did he owe his life? Nat, it had to be Nat. Only Nat. If only he could be sure.

"Wes?" Nat shook his arm.

Let me in.

Wes stumbled back from Nat.

Why? he said to the lady. *What do you want with me?*

In the distance, they heard a soldier shouting into a radio, calling for reinforcements. A drone hovered above them, a second approached. There would be more on the way.

Nat looked up, brought her hands together, and clapped once more. The drones smashed into each other, as surely as if she'd flown one into the next. Burning debris fell from the sky, plummeting into the city around them.

But when the smoke cleared there were only that many more drones—and they were coming right at them. In the distance, the soldiers had regrouped; they'd be on them in a heartbeat.

Nat would never have the strength to defeat them all. Not after the combat she'd already seen today. Wes looked around, desperate for a new plan.

An escape route. A safe place to hide out, even. But with every moment, more soldiers returned, and he knew that their chances of survival were only shrinking.

Let me in, the voice said again. *I'm all you have.*

He ignored it. Ignored her.

"Let's go," Wes said, backing toward Nat. They needed to run, to get away before the soldiers spotted them.

"Where?" Nat asked. Blinking against the smoke and looking through the burned-out streets, she saw soldiers and tanks everywhere. No sign of their crew or where they had gone.

"Good question." Where could they run? It was all he could do to stay alive between the flying rocks and bullets and glass.

"Over here!" Wes heard a shout, and saw Shakes pick off a soldier who had his gun trained on Nat. Then a second soldier fell, and a third.

"I got your back," shouted Roark, heaving a glass window into the knees of a fourth. The brave members of their crew had returned to join the fray.

Shakes kept firing, while Roark and Brendon smashed debris into the soldiers' legs, tripping them up. Liannan made the wind howl and screech, sending great bolts of lightning into the crowd, flinging blinding waves of dirt into the eyes of Nat and Wes's attackers.

Nat redoubled her offensive, sending guns and soldiers flying away, though with less and less effect. She looked so tired now that she could barely stand.

Wes picked up his weapon and fired until the piece clicked helplessly in his hand. He was out of ammo.

The enemy pressed forward.

As it did, Wes felt the voice in his head again. *Let me in, you foolish boy.* The lady was insistent now. *You are wasting time.*

"Nat," Wes shouted. "Run! Get them out of here, I'll hold them off—"

"No! We're not leaving you!"

"Nat, please—"

Just then, a soldier clocked Wes on the head with a two-by-four, and smacked him to the ground while he tried to reload his gun.

Nat faltered, her foot caught on a broken steel beam. She fell to the pavement, her leg wrenched.

That was it, the moment the crowd had been waiting for—and Wes saw right then that he was never the target, that it had always been her.

"NAT!" Wes yelled, as the soldiers leapt upon her, one after another, burying her beneath them, the snow falling on all of them. He threw himself at the pile, pushing through her assailants, but his back was throbbing from where the glass had pierced his skin, and his head felt as if someone were splitting it with an axe. His vision began to blur, and he was staggering.

A stone struck him in the jaw, and he thought he felt the bone break. A second hit sent him reeling, falling to the ground. Someone kicked him in the gut, and he spit blood, while another foot, another fist, and another piece of glass shattered upon him.

We're both going to die, Wes thought. *Right here, today. At least we're going to die together.* He managed to open his eyes wide enough to see the fate of his crew. It was no better.

Shakes struggled to fight off three soldiers. Liannan was in shackles, a gun held to her brow. Roark lay facedown in the dirt, unconscious. Brendon fell to his knees, a pistol shoved up his mouth.

Worst of all, Nat was hidden beneath a herd of soldiers, each of them taking turns kicking her and knocking her on the head with their rifles.

The lady had no more patience, not for him. *Let me in, foolish boy! NOW!*

Fine! Wes screamed to the voice in his head. *Whatever you want, whatever you think you can do to help, you need to do it now!*

Open! the lady said.

Wes stopped fighting her and felt her rummaging around his mind. Too late to close it now.

I'm coming, said the voice. *Hold on.*

Wes looked over to see the soldiers had taken Nat prisoner, and now they turned their guns on Wes and his crew.

"Throw it down," said an officer, pointing to the gun.

Wes tossed it to the ground. It was empty anyway. Shakes did the same. They weren't going to fight their way out of this one, not this time.

There were just too many of the enemy to fight, and all of them were armed, ready to shoot, trigger-happy.

It was really over.

"Against the wall," said the officer, gesturing with the butt of his rifle. "All of you, line up!"

Wes and his crew were herded against the alley wall with the rest of the marked prisoners. He knew what came next, and it wasn't good. The soldiers made them all stand in line, preparing a firing squad.

Summary execution, thought Wes. It would all be over in a minute.

Hold on, said the voice in his head. But Wes was done holding on; there was no more time for that. He could hardly open his eyes—a bruise had forced one shut, the other was bloodshot. Nat looked over at him, shaking her head. She couldn't speak; she could barely stand. She was spent, nothing more to give. They were done.

He reached out for her hand and she took it. With her other hand, she took Liannan's. Liannan took Shakes's, who took Roark's, who held Brendon's.

Wes leaned forward. "See you in the next life, my friends."

"Been an honor," said Roark.

"Been something, all right." Shakes smiled.

"Rather leave with friends than live with snakes," Brendon agreed.

"Besides," said Liannan, "Farouk is waiting."

"Agreed," Nat whispered. Wes squeezed her hand tighter. They would die together. All of them.

"FIRE!" Gunshots exploded in the smoky air, echoing like thunder through the cavernous streets of New Kandy.

This is it— Wes braced himself, but the bullets shattered in midair.

He waited for death but it did not come. He expected a hail of bullets, readied himself for the pain, but there was nothing, and he remained intact, whole.

The gun smoke that remained was thick and gray, and it stung his eyes, clouding up in a great wave in front of him.

Even through the smoke, he could see that the soldiers were gone.

In their place was a circle of sunlight, so bright it washed out the streets of the White Temple around it.

I'm here, said the voice.

All around him, the dark alley filled with an incandescent light. *Some kind of tear in the fabric of reality,* Wes thought. *It's a miracle. Or the end of the world. Or . . .*

It's her.

"A portal!" cried Nat, who recognized the pattern, as snow-filled air began to swirl around them, creating a funnel, the wind kicking up debris until the space resolved into a shimmering window to another place and time.

Not just any place and time.

Vallonis.

Wes thought he heard birdsong, a river rushing in the distance. It was strange to see such beauty in the heart of so much destruction. *There are other worlds than these,* he'd read once in a book a long time ago. Hadn't he?

It was hard to remember now, what was real and what was not. What was a memory, and what was a dream.

The lady in white appeared at the mouth of the portal.

Did I dream her? She wore a shade of white so pure that it sparkled like a star, so pristine that it had no color at all; it was translucent, like crystal draped over her slender frame.

Nat, standing by his side, gasped.

The lady's face was ageless and unlined, and Wes remembered her as if it had been only yesterday that Eliza had been stolen away.

Then the woman smiled at him, and when she spoke, just as he expected, her voice and the voice in his head were one and the same.

"I am Nineveh, Queen of Vallonis. Come."

7

SO THIS WAS NINEVEH.

Nat had never met the ruler of Vallonis, not in all the months she lived in the Blue. Faix had been bringing her to Apis, to meet the Queen, when Nat abandoned her training to try to save her friends. She was awestruck and overwhelmed and, for a moment, relieved. Someone was here to help, someone was here to save them. The Queen had arrived, and they would be safe. Nat never realized how much she needed that until now. She never thought of herself as anyone who needed rescue, but the Queen's presence stilled her fear. Nineveh was not just the Queen of Vallonis; to Nat, she was the living embodiment of it—pure, sacred, incorruptible magic.

She breathed deeply. They were not alone in the their fight. Help had come. She looked to Wes, expecting to see relief, but his face was pale, his eyes uncertain.

"What is it?" she asked.

Wes was moving along the wall, one step, then another, retreating into the smoky haze, away from the lady in white. He shared none of Nat's relief, not a bit of her excitement.

"What's going on?" she asked, raising her voice a little. They should be greeting the Queen, exchanging pleasantries and titles, or whatever you did when you met your sovereign. Nat didn't know. But Wes looked like he wanted to run. And Nat wasn't sure what she felt. Something was definitely wrong. Nineveh stood twenty or thirty feet away. She was coming closer and Wes was backing away from her.

"Nat," he whispered, urging her to join him.

She went to his side, a bit reluctantly. The smoke enveloped them, making it seem as if the two of them were alone.

"I don't know about this," he said.

"What do you mean?" she asked, startled that he did not feel the same as she did. Of course Wes would be wary, he was only being cautious, but she had to convince him otherwise. Nineveh was only here to help, Nat was sure of it. So what was wrong with Wes? She gestured to the battle that raged on every side of them, the sound of bombs echoing all over the city. "Look around you. This is our only way out."

"Yeah, but I'm telling you, I have a bad feeling about this," Wes said. He chewed his lip, his eyes flickering back in the direction of the Queen of Vallonis. She approached, greeting the others in their crew. Liannan was kneeling already. "I mean, it's hard to explain, but I know she used her connection to me to get here, and my gut says something's up."

Nat silently absorbed this information. She had a feeling Wes wanted to say more, so she held her tongue and her arguments for now.

Wes sighed and scratched the scar on his face. "The Queen—whoever she is—I've met her before . . . I'm pretty sure she was the one who stole Eliza. She took her, that night."

He was confirming what she already knew, that Eliza had been taken by the rulers of Vallonis. Nat recalled Eliza's bitterness toward Faix in the White Temple, her disdain for him and the Queen. *I called them Mother and Father,* Eliza had said.

"Nineveh took your sister because she thought your sister was the one who could help them break the spell and cast a new one," said Nat. "And when Eliza realized she wasn't the one, she turned against them."

"It still wasn't right, what she did. She shouldn't have taken Eliza away. My whole life, I was haunted by her voice, her face, what happened that night. And then, just now, when I was dead, or when I thought I was—when I was lying next to you on the deck of that ferry—I heard her voice in my head again. This time, she said that she'd made a mistake. I think I was the one she wanted all along."

"Because you are the true child of Vallonis," Nat said. She had seen the strength of his power, how he had been able to defeat Eliza and her illusions. His ability to dispel magic was a powerful gift.

"Whatever I am, I don't know what she wants from me now. Why she's here. And I'm not sure we should do what she wants us to."

His face was so anguished that Nat was torn. She didn't want to doubt the Queen's intentions, but she didn't want to dismiss Wes's wariness either.

The Queen had her reasons for stealing Eliza Wesson— her actions had broken a family and jeopardized the fate of the entire world—but was that Nineveh's fault? And what if Nineveh was only here to fix what was broken? Now that the Queen knew Wes was the child she had sought all along, didn't it follow that she would act on it?

Nat had to make Wes understand. Nineveh was on their side, she wanted what they wanted—to make things right.

The crew jostled them. "Come on, man, there's no way out of here but through there," said Shakes, pointing to the portal. "What are we waiting for? We need to get these people and our butts out of here."

The Queen waited at the portal, gesturing for all of them to approach.

Liannan was already at the entrance, but she hesitated, looking back at Wes and Nat. She was the Queen's subject, but she was also one of their team now. She put a hand on Shakes's arm to tell him to wait. They would do what Wes told them to.

"Something's off," Wes said abruptly. "I don't think we should go. We'll find another way."

The smallmen looked longingly at the open portal. All around them was smoke and death, but through the portal they could see blue skies and peaceful vistas. Roark could barely see through one swollen eye. Brendon had a massive bruise on his forehead. "Whatever you say, boss," he said. Roark nodded.

Nat admired their loyalty, but she had to make them see what was right in front of them. Hope. Refuge. Safety. "If we don't go with her, where will we go?" she asked Wes.

"We could try the mountains," he said. "The original plan. Find another boat, get out of here, get back home."

Home? Oh, he meant New Vegas. But Vallonis was her home, and home was so very close right now.

"If we go through the mountains, not all of us will survive," she said, meaning the remaining prisoners. "We're risking everyone's lives."

Nobody argued with her, not even Wes, because she was right.

Nat weighed the options in front of them, knowing a fresh band of attackers were sure to appear at any moment. New Kandy was burning; she could taste the grease and the gunpowder. Every part of her body ached. She trusted Wes, but he didn't know the workings of the Blue.

She placed a hand on his cheek, looked deep into his eyes. "Vallonis will protect us—and these prisoners." She motioned to the ragged collection of survivors still following them. "She is their Queen. These are her people. She's here for them."

Wes placed his hand on hers and squeezed. But then he pulled away, ran his fingers through his messy hair, and shook his head. "I just don't trust her," he said. "I can't."

Nat turned to look back at Nineveh. The Queen of Vallonis, who stood in front of the only escape plan available to them, Nineveh, the lady in white, who had appeared at their darkest hour, a savior, a beacon, who offered refuge.

To Wes, Nineveh was an enemy, a stranger. He was right to question her motives because of what happened in the past, but Nineveh was Faix's Queen, and Faix had been her friend and mentor. The one who had taught her how to control her power, the one who had taught her the mysteries of magic. Nat would put her trust in Faix, and in her faith in Vallonis.

So she turned once more to the boy she loved, the one from whom she drew her strength, the one with doubt in his eyes. "I can handle her. You don't have to trust her. Trust me."

Wes took a deep breath.

She knew he trusted her with his crew, with his heart, with his life. She had to make him understand this was their only way out. It was time to go, no time to hesitate. They would handle whatever came after, if she was wrong about this. But she wasn't wrong.

"Trust me," she repeated.

Wes rubbed his eyes with his fists. When he put his hands away, she saw that they were still red. "I do trust you. Always." He kissed her forehead. "Okay. Let's do it."

Nat inhaled sharply, relieved that it would soon be over. Soon, they would be back in Vallonis, away from this carnage.

Wes took her hand and together they walked to the portal. Through the smoke they went, hurrying as best they could. The doorway to Vallonis looked bigger than it had from a distance. It made a sound like a hurricane that made it hard to speak, hard to think. The Queen waited at the base of the portal, silent, unmoving. Wes came closer.

He turned toward Nineveh and gave her the slightest nod.

The Queen gestured to the entrance with one delicate, white-sleeved arm, and moved aside. It was all so strange, almost like a dream. She was just standing there, silent as marble, gesturing to the doorway.

With a flash of light and a great roar, the first of the marked prisoners walked through the portal, and disappeared into Vallonis. Liannan stood at the door, frantically calling for them to hurry through it. There had been hundreds in the White Temple, but there were only a handful of survivors now. They gawked at Nineveh and hurried past. The Queen kept her chin raised high. When they were all safe, Liannan followed, Shakes at her side. The smallmen were next.

Nat stood at the portal's edge. Warm air kissed her face, the scent of orange and jasmine heady and sweet. She couldn't wait to go home. She couldn't wait for this bleak chapter in their life to be over.

Wes tugged her coat. "Come on," he said, anxiously looking over his shoulder at the tanks that were headed their way.

"You first," she said. She was the drakonrydder of Vallonis; she would be last to leave.

He reached for her hand. "We'll go together."

They turned to the portal, but the Queen stopped them, moving with unnatural speed to block their path. "She cannot pass," said Nineveh, pointing at Nat. Her face was as cold as the words she had spoken. "She stays behind."

"Me?" asked Nat, not quite believing what she was hearing. She stared right at the Queen, but it was as if Nineveh did not see her; the Queen's gaze pierced right through Nat. "But why?"

The Queen addressed Wes, as if she were loath to speak directly to Nat. "She is not welcome in Vallonis."

Wes was right, Nat thought. Something is wrong with the

Queen. Something is wrong—and a terrible thought occurred to her. What if the something that was wrong—was Nat herself? What did the Queen know? Why did she refuse her entrance?

Nat looked at Wes, suddenly fearful, but the doubt in his eyes was completely gone now, replaced by a calm decisiveness. "I'm not leaving her," he told the Queen. "She comes with me. She's with us."

He tilted his chin at the Queen. "Move it."

Nineveh remained where she was, implacable, unruffled. "The girl stays behind."

"Wes . . . ," said Nat hesitantly. "Maybe I should . . ."

"I said, move," Wes repeated, his hand still holding Nat's. He squeezed it to assure her he wouldn't leave her, but Nat wanted to tell him that maybe they were in the wrong. Maybe they should listen to Nineveh. If the Queen didn't want her in Vallonis, there had to be a reason. Nat felt she had to do something, because Wes looked like he was going to throttle the Queen, no matter how powerful her magic might be.

There were only the three of them left, and the ground shook from another explosion. "Look, this is no time to argue! Let us through!" She could hear the roar of the drones above, the sound of more tanks headed their way. When she arrived, Nineveh had pushed back the soldiers, she'd cleared a path for everyone to enter the portal, but now the soldiers had returned.

"Move! I'm not leaving her!" Wes yelled. Nat knew what

he was thinking. Their friends were already across the portal, and there was no other way out of the burning city. The clop of heavy boots striking concrete echoed all around them. A soldier shouted orders in the distance.

"She is forbidden to enter," Nineveh said.

But I am the Protector of Vallonis, thought Nat.

This time, the Queen looked directly at Nat, her ice-blue eyes boring into Nat's green ones. Her voice was cold as the air around them. Colder. "Vallonis has no protector. Only a pretender."

The words stung and found their mark. Nat stared at the Queen in disbelief. But in an instant, she understood why she was cast out. She saw the grief on the Queen's face. It hung there, heavy and motionless, like a death mask. She might as well have been carved of ceremonial clay.

Of course. A death mask. That's exactly what it is. It's Faix.

Nat had brought death to Faix, the Queen's consort. She blamed Nat for his death. The loss had crushed Nat herself, leaving her empty and lost. She could only imagine what it had been like for the Queen.

"Go," Nat told Wes, pulling him aside to beseech him to save himself at least. "Leave me. I don't belong there. I know why she doesn't want me. Because of Faix, because Faix is dead, and it's all my fault."

"No! I'm not going without you. Never." He tightened his grip on her hand. There were soldiers in the street, coming closer. "What happened to Faix wasn't your fault. He knew the risks, he knew what Eliza had become, and he went to her freely. Faix gave his life for yours. He wouldn't want this."

"Let him go," said the Queen, her cold gaze resting upon Nat once more.

Nat winced as she heard the Queen's cold voice in her head.

Let the boy go.

You will kill them all.

You will bring death to everyone around you, death to all whom you love.

If you stay with him, you will destroy him.

Nat squeezed her eyes shut, but she couldn't keep from hearing the truth in Nineveh's words. She was no protector. She couldn't protect her friends. She couldn't save Faix, couldn't do anything while Farouk was decimated right in front of her.

How many more would die from her mistakes?

Nat pulled her hand away from Wes's and moved away from the portal. "You should go. The crew—they need you. I can take care of myself, you know I can. Don't worry about me. I'll meet you on the other side." But the other side of what? How would Wes find her? She knew that the odds were against her, that without her drakon and their crew she would never make it out of New Kandy and that she would never see him again.

She also knew she couldn't let him stay.

A soldier's voice shot through the air. "You there, you three. Put your hands up." Someone was telling them to surrender. It was time to make a decision, to stay or to go.

If he stayed here with her, he'd die, too—and that would be worse than her own death. Seeing him almost die in her arms today had only made her more certain. He had to go.

And she had to say something to make him *move*. "I'll find you, I swear I will."

8

IF NAT THOUGHT WES WOULD BE ABLE TO leave while she remained in this burning city, she didn't understand him at all. She wouldn't have a chance without him—and he wouldn't have a life, without her. He wouldn't even bother trying.

As if to better make the point, a whole battalion crashed into the alley, guns blazing. The soldier who told them to put down their hands just shook his head. He'd tried to get them to surrender. Now they'd have to fight.

When Nat had pulled away, Wes had been taken aback by her actions. For a moment he thought it meant Nat had found a reason to slip away from him, to leave him again, because for an awful second he thought that maybe she'd changed her mind about him.

But now he realized she was leaving him because she loved him too much. She would sacrifice her safety for his, no matter what it cost.

His heart swelled and he wanted to tell her there was no

need for such a terrible sacrifice. They would be together, always. He had sworn an oath to her.

Nat was slowly backing away, and Wes knew if he didn't act quickly, she would soon disappear into the smoky, destroyed city.

I'll meet you on the other side? I'll find you? What kind of crap promise was that?

They were together now, and nothing would separate them. Wes glared at the Queen, at the person who had stolen his sister and who was threatening his dearest love. He glared at the soldiers who surrounded them. "I don't care whether Vallonis wants her or not, I do, and she's coming with me." Without warning, he grabbed Nat's hand, pulling her back to his side, while at the same time he flung his body forward, meaning to jump through the portal.

But something barred his way. A spell, some kind of magical barrier, blocked the entrance. He should have known there was no forcing their way past this door.

Wish I had the same luck keeping the White Lady out of my head.

To make things worse, a bullet shattered against the barrier, sending shrapnel flying in all directions.

"The pretender is not welcome in Vallonis," Nineveh repeated calmly, as bullets began to rain upon them. "I will not allow it."

Wes put a finger in the lady's face. "Let us through this door or it's your death as well, Queenie."

Nineveh stared him down, impassive.

He didn't care. "In fact, I'll make sure that all we all die here. Whatever you want from me, I'm no use to you dead."

"Is that so?" The Queen remained expressionless. "But you have already proven useful."

She did not appear to be moved by his threat—or by the bullets that whizzed in the air or the soldiers that filled the streets around where they stood. Her face was as cool as white marble. There was no sweat on her brow, and not a trace of fear in her eyes.

It's like she's not real, Wes thought. *Like she's untouchable.* She reminded him of someone he knew, and the nagging feeling of doubt returned.

Nineveh's long hair fluttered in the wind as a hail of bullets hurtled through the air, then broke upon some sort of magic aura that seemed to protect every bit of her pale skin. The shells burst and shattered in the air around her, leaving her unscathed. Her magic was keeping the soldiers at bay.

"Wes, please—it's all right," said Nat, tears in her voice. "You have to go. Please, or you'll die here."

"I've already died twice before," he said, smiling down at her. "Somehow I'm not worried."

Nat flushed. "I can't fix this one. Listen to her."

"I am, but I don't like what she's saying."

As if to prove his point, the Queen spoke again. "The pretender belongs to the gray world," she commanded, her face placid. "She stays here."

"To hell with that," said Wes, "and you know what? To hell with you too. Ice it."

The Queen blinked. She faltered only for a moment, but Wes saw the façade slip, ever so slightly.

So I can rattle you, he thought. It gave him an idea. A simple one, but an idea, nonetheless. He was still weak from the first time he'd used his power, weak from his many wounds, but he didn't care. If one façade could drop, perhaps another could.

Either way, he had to try. It was time to go, it was time to put a stop to this nonsense. Even as he thought the words, a bullet whizzed past his nose, and another grazed his shoulder, drawing a line of blood.

We're running out of time.

"I'll find another way," said Nat. "Please, Wes. Just go."

"No, this is the only way." He brought her hand up to his lips and kissed it, wondering as he did so whether they would ever survive the day, whether they would survive to live their lives together. He had so many plans for them. So many dreams he hadn't even begun to share.

Then he slid his arm around her waist, pulling her tight, pulling her closer to him, so that she couldn't run away again.

Nat whispered in his ear so softly he had to strain to listen. "You heard what the Queen said. She doesn't want me. I don't belong in Vallonis." Her voice was so soft and defeated.

"It doesn't matter, because you belong with me," he said, nuzzling her so that she leaned into him, and he could rest his chin on her head. They fit so well together he wished he had more time to enjoy it.

The Queen regarded them thoughtfully, but appeared unmoved as before.

Wes moved his lips to Nat's ear. "On my count—one—two—"

"Wes—wait—what are you doing—" she whispered, agitated.

"NOW!"

Before Nat could protest, Wes tightened his grasp on her waist and rolled them both right into the portal, at once diving and falling and slipping past the Queen. They flew into the bright light of the doorway at full speed, and as Wes threw the whole weight of his body—and Nat's—into the great bubble of nothingness in front of them, he turned the full force of his mind toward the barrier before the portal.

He had used his magic to dispel Eliza's illusions once. Could he use it on the Queen? Could he break whatever magic prevented them from entering the portal?

Time to find out.

As they fell, Wes focused on the invisible obstacle, tearing it to shreds with his mind. *You are nothing—meaningless—weak.*

His power sent shock waves rippling through the air. The great and hazy doorway undulated, sending a stream of energy rippling in all directions. The Queen's magic had not simply faltered—it was utterly destroyed. She was made of magic, and her spells were a part of her. To break the spell, he needed to break Nineveh. When her magic fell, when he struck down her spell, the Queen cried out, falling to her knees in a fit of anguished cries.

I didn't want to hurt anyone, but she gave me no choice. I couldn't just leave Nat.

The portal opened and the Queen collapsed, her entire body shaking. She looked up at Wes in confusion. Was this the first time she'd met someone who could match her strength?

Maybe. She flashed him a look of shock, then recovered as her lips curled into a snarl.

Wes ignored her, tightening his hold around Nat as they fell through the doorway and dropped, spinning into the light beyond.

9

SHE FELT HIS HAND SLIP AWAY FROM her waist as their bodies came apart at the force of his magic pulverizing the door. *Wes!* she cried, panicked and afraid to lose him again so soon. She had tried to hold on to him, but the strength of the magic was too much. Now she was alone, spinning, dropping, and racing toward oblivion. *From oblivion to oblivion—from world to world—from gray to blue.*

Nobody else but Wes would have even dared to try to break into Vallonis like that. And not even Wes could have prepared her for how it would feel when they'd actually done it. The force of his power, the sensation of falling. The rage of a broken Queen behind them.

As Nat felt the solid world drop out from beneath their feet, her panic was soon replaced by fearlessness and wonder.

All around her was light, a million stars bursting into life, hurtling across space and time, the universe all around and the universe inside her; she was the universe. She was something out of nothing.

Magic.

And just as quickly as she had entered the infinite, she was already on the other side, having left one world and fallen into the other, back in the land she was sworn to protect. The clear-skied domain of Vallonis, the fabled *Blue* to which she had once fled, took shape in front of her, as if it were stitching itself together into reality from the air and light surrounding her.

So beautiful, it made her heart ache, except her heart was already aching. In fact, it was pounding in her chest, her fear of what the Queen had told her ringing in her ears. *You will bring death to everyone around you, death to all whom you love. If you stay with him, you will destroy him.*

What did that mean?

When she was a captive at MacArthur, when she had been a prisoner of the RSA, she had also been their favorite weapon.

A weapon of darkness.

A vessel of rage.

Nineveh was the Queen of Vallonis and she had rejected Nat. *Vallonis has no protector,* the Queen had said. *Only a pretender.*

I'm a monster, she had told Wes once.

Weapon. Monster. Pretender.

What am I? Who am I truly?

But then she had no time to think about it further, because the land had become real, the dust flying and the rock crumbling and the green growth springing beneath her toes.

And then she was there. *Here.* Standing straight and tall, back in the land that she had sworn to defend.

"Nat! Where are you?" She heard his voice before she saw him. *Wes*. She ran to him and flew into his arms.

As impossible as it had once seemed, they had escaped the city of the White Temple. They were here, and they were saved.

Nat blinked her eyes at the bright sun of the fabled land. Wes was by her side, shaking the melting snowflakes out of his hair, looking dazed but alive. He'd done it. She rested her head on his chest, listened to the steady beat of his heart.

"Look," he said.

The rest of the team—down to every last one of the prisoners they had rescued—were not far away. Liannan was breathing deeply into a handful of honeysuckle. Shakes lay back in the solid dirt. Brendon tried to help Roark out of a tangle of brambles where he seemed to have fallen.

The grass was soft under their feet, the air clean and fresh. It was too good to be true. She was home.

Except it wasn't much of a homecoming.

"What have you done?" a horrified voice called out from the meadow. From every direction they emerged, from behind rolling hills, from the dense groves of exotic trees, from the tangled crags that lay in the distance, from the sky, riding winged horses. The sylphs of Vallonis came with their golden hair glowing and their robes of deep green and silver, shining in the pale morning light. They came with their mouths gaping, eyes wide, staring up at the sky. "What have you done?" they asked again. There was shock in the voices, horror.

"Nothing we could avoid," Nat said.

"We just took a fall," Wes added.

"No." A violet-eyed elder shook his head and repeated the question, pointing upward. "What have you done?"

They looked up.

The portal had been ripped wide open. It was now a jagged black hole in the sky, extending all the way down to the earth—nearly as large and as wide as a tank that barreled through the woods, rolling over everything in its path.

Exactly like a tank, in fact.

Because Wes and Nat and the others hadn't escaped the war. The war had followed them to the Blue. For years the RSA had sought a doorway into Vallonis, and now they had one.

Soldiers blasted their guns, claiming victory. Above them, the horizon seethed with mechanical drones.

Liannan screamed in horror.

Wes cursed like the soldier he had been.

"Nat, I swear—I didn't know! I didn't mean to—" he cried, his voice already hoarse.

Nat stared at the sky, at the battle that was brewing above them. *No, no, no, no. What have we done? Nineveh was right. I should have known. I should have realized what would happen. This is all my doing. The Queen was right. She was right about me.*

"Where is Nineveh?" the same sylph demanded.

Nat shook her head miserably. "I don't know. Didn't she come through after we did?" But Nat knew she hadn't. She had seen the Queen fall to her knees. It had taken all of Wes's strength to break the Queen's magic. There was no way he could have known what would happen next. He'd only tried to save her, to bring Nat with him, to save the one he loved. But to do that had taken all of his strength, and that power had torn the portal open, leaving it vulnerable to their enemies.

"I didn't know . . . I didn't think . . . It's all my fault. I did this," said Wes, utterly stricken.

"No, I did," she said. "You did nothing wrong." There was no doubt in Nat's mind that this was her fault; she had caused this. The Queen had forbidden her to enter. She had brought death to Vallonis. She, who had sworn to protect Vallonis, had as much as doomed the place.

I am nothing but a pretender.

A weapon.

A monster.

A tree exploded in the distance. The impact was so powerful that the sylphs themselves were tossed into the air by the force of the explosion.

In the distance, a castle tower crumbled when a second shell struck its midsection. Now they watched as artillery fire lit the forest. Ancient trees burst into flame. Destruction surrounded them, once again.

As the skies overhead filled with drones, as the winged horses of Vallonis circled and acrid smoke drifted through the sunshine, Nat knew this would be the last stand for the Blue. There was no going back from here as the two worlds were colliding and the corruption was far too great to hold back now. Maybe it was inevitable, maybe it was her fault, but nothing would have stopped this from happening someday.

Even so, she didn't mean to go down without a fight.

If she was a weapon and a monster, she was their weapon, their monster. She didn't pretend to be anything else. All she'd ever wanted was to come home, to be in a place where she belonged.

"Tell us what to do," said Wes, his voice cutting through her thoughts. "Tell us how we can stop this."

He didn't have to say it, because she knew what he was really saying. *You are not alone. This is our fight as well.*

Nat felt a rush of adrenaline and a fierce, angry joy. She motioned for the crew and the rest of the sylphs to gather around her.

"If we cannot close the gate, then we must defend it!" she cried. "We must defend our land! Sound the call, spread the word! To arms!"

Wes threw her a sword and she raised it high.

The sylphs were already in motion, meeting fire with blazing arrows of their own, diving through the air on winged horses while they called on lightning to strike their foes. Soon, it was difficult to see them in their cloud of smoke.

Nat ran to the head of the charge as more sylphs and smallmen emerged from their homes in the forests and the mountains to join the battle. Wes grabbed a thick-bladed axe from a passing cart and tossed it to Shakes, stealing another for himself. Roark found a blade from the cart, while Brendon took one off a riderless horse left tied to a waiting tree.

Liannan and Nat began to work their magic, and one by one, the people of Vallonis rallied to its defense.

If this was the end of their world, they would not go quietly.

Her blood running high, Nat threw herself into the fray. She had once been was the protector of Vallonis, and she had fought to save this place. Now Vallonis would fight at her side.

In the midst of the sylphs was one who stood above the rest, who was taller than any other, and fairer, too. He wore armor that looked like steel, but it shone with an ethereal light, an otherworldly glow so intense it made Nat shade her eyes. He wore a cloak of purple, deep as dried blood, and his hair was the color of snow. He was drau. One of the formidable. The feared heartrenders of Vallonis.

"Rally to me," the drau ordered, his voice thundering across the green and rolling downs, and all at once, he soared to the sky, as his horse unfurled its glorious white wings, leading a flying cavalry through the skies to chase down the drones. "Rain death on our enemies!"

"Who is that?" Nat asked, blinking at the sight.

"My father!" said Liannan, her eyes shining. "He's a general in the Queen's army."

Wes raised an eyebrow at the old man and punched Shakes on the shoulder. "Good luck with that man," he muttered under his breath.

Shakes whistled.

"Come on!" Wes cried, running after the army battalion, Shakes and the smallmen right after him.

The battle raged on all sides of them. Black-winged drones made circles in the sky, raking the sylph army with bullets. The air was hazy, full of smoke and gunfire, but the sylphs of Vallonis did not waver in their resolve or retreat—they pressed onward.

Yet the army assault was just as relentless. They were bringing in the big guns now, rolling in whatever they could fit through the portal—tanks, artillery. Even the air was starting to cool as the bitter wind of New Kandy swept in through the open door.

Defending the portal would only take them so far, Nat realized. They had to stop more of the RSA from entering. The military had a seemingly limitless supply of drones, and if they kept sending them through, there was no hope at all for victory.

Nat knew what she had to do, and she forced herself to do it before she changed her mind.

"WES!" she screamed, pushing through the melee, looking for his dark head among all the gold and silver ones. "We need to close the portal! Find the Queen! She's the only one who can close this thing!"

"Where is she?" he asked, hacking his way through crowd, waving the smoke away from his face.

"She's still back there! On the other side!"

Wes hesitated, and she knew it was because he did not want to leave her. Not after everything they had been through; but this was different from before, there was too much on the line now. He had to understand that she needed to stay here to fight and she needed him to go back to New Kandy to find Nineveh.

"I guess I don't have much of a choice, do I?" He smiled wanly.

She shook her head, returned his smile with a stronger one of her own. "Please, find her. Bring her back here. I'll be right here when you return. I promise."

He would come back to her, alive and whole. He *would*.

She willed it to happen. It was the only way she could let him walk away.

Wes gave her one last lingering glance before disappearing back through the portal.

Nat's heart went with him.

10

WITHOUT ANOTHER LOOK BACK, WES tumbled through the portal and onto the streets of New Kandy. A freezing wind blew, and he shivered at the cold and the snow that was falling around him. He shuddered when a drone streaked through the sky above. All around him flames crackled and engines roared. He heard soldiers shouting, coming closer. A shot rang out. Someone must have seen him jump back through the portal. He saw the soldiers coming toward him, so he fled the area around the portal, hurrying to conceal himself in the haze of smoke and dust that covered the city.

From behind a snow-covered mound of debris, he saw men rushing toward the portal, gathering in lines, readying themselves for the invasion. Where was Nineveh? How could he find her in this chaos?

"Nineveh!" he yelled, his voice hoarse as he tried to make himself heard above the sound of gunfire and explosions. "Nineveh! Where are you? Vallonis needs you!"

Thinking of the war that had come to the Blue made him ill. He had done that. He had broken the portal, had torn a rent in the fabric of space and time, had let in the dark. No matter what Nat said, this was his mess and now he had to fix it. Fast. Before everything was destroyed.

He'd only just learned of his power and how to use it. When he broke one of Nineveh's spells, he hadn't known that it would affect all of them. He hadn't known that tearing down the spell that kept Nat from entering the doorway would also disrupt the spell that kept the portal open. How could he know? All of this was new to him. He had no teacher, no peers. For all he knew he was the only person in the world who had these particular powers and he barely understood them. He was dangerous and desperate, and he'd only wanted to save Nat. *I've made a mess of things, but now I'm going to fix it.*

Peering over the debris toward the portal, he saw what looked like a crack in the fabric of the worlds, a great and terrible gash. *I have to close it, but I don't think I can do that with magic.* He sensed that only Nineveh could do that, so he strengthened his resolve to find her.

The streets were piled high with snow and ice-covered debris. He circled around the block, ducking through burned-out buildings, avoiding the foot patrols. He ran through the burning streets till he stopped and caught his breath.

This was no way to find her.

This wasn't how she'd found *him*.

The Queen had used their connection to locate him the first time, and Wes realized he should try to do the same. He just had to go back there. To the night of the fire. To the night Nineveh appeared to take away one of the twins and Eliza was stolen.

Wes closed his eyes.

And went back home.

When they were little, no one believed they were related. It was an odd thing for twins, but features that were pleasing and symmetrical on his face were awkward and elongated on hers. Eliza had been a difficult child; he had few memories of his sister that didn't include her scowling or crying or angry. His parents called her colicky or worried she'd been born with ice disease. But Eliza was completely healthy yet fully wretched at the same time.

At six years old, he knew that there was something wrong with Eliza and that there was something terrible about her. The fires she started, and the way she made you see things that weren't there, feel things that weren't real—she messed with your mind. She was twisted, as if there was something inside her that was eating her up.

It was magic, he realized now. He had it, too, but he'd suppressed it, didn't touch it, never explored that side of himself, that part of his nature. It was too foreign and too frightening to contemplate.

For those who were marked by magic were marked for death. Inside and out. If they weren't taken away by the RSA, they became madmen who rotted in the streets. He realized that the effort to deny what was inside him had led to his temporary blindness, the tremors in his hands. But since using his power, his ailments were gone, and he was fully inhabiting his body in a way he hadn't before.

The power within him made his heart beat a little faster, made his senses a bit sharper. He felt strangely fulfilled. He'd never had much of a career after leaving the service. He was just a runner, a guy who took odd jobs just to get by. He raced cars and smuggled people and goods. It was nothing to be proud of, not a living. He'd done whatever he needed to do to earn enough heat credits to keep warm, but he wasn't that guy anymore. All that felt like a hundred years ago, a different life—a different person.

No more. He knew who he was, the power he had. And maybe that power scared him a bit. He'd taken on the Queen and won—how much more could he do? And what damage could he cause if he accidently misused that power? He needed to be more careful, but how could he? Everywhere he went there were soldiers and magic folk, and all of them had it out for him. Wes was starting lose track of how many times he'd nearly lost his life and how many people had been taken from him.

Eliza. All of this started the night Eliza was taken. The road that led here, started years ago in a bedroom with his sister.

When Nineveh appeared that night, Wes had let Eliza step forward and had done nothing while the Queen took her away.

I was mistaken, Nineveh had told him earlier.

But what if the mistake was his?

What if he had never let Nineveh take his sister, his twin? What if he had fought to keep Eliza at home? He was only a boy then, but he should have done something. Maybe he should have taken her place.

Especially since he was the one Nineveh wanted all along. Eliza had mentioned being unable to break the mist around the tower that held the spell. Was that what he was supposed to do?

The Queen had looked deep into his thoughts and had used the connection she had forged that night to find him again ten years later. Wes focused on that night, on Nineveh's voice, and willed himself to her side.

When he found her, the Queen was standing where they had left her, by the alleyway, in front of the portal. The soldiers were rushing past her, diving through the doorway to Vallonis, carrying heavy armaments, rockets, and rifles. The portal shimmered as they dove through its swirling surface. There were soldiers all around her, but none of them noticed the Queen. No one stopped, raised a rifle, or paused to ask who she was, what was she doing there. Had she cloaked herself somehow? Was that how he had missed her before?

He was hiding among the piles of snow, concealing himself from the soldiers, wondering how he could approach the Queen, when she spoke to him in his thoughts: *The portal is open to all. You broke the seal,* she said. *It is done. The end has come to Vallonis.* She left the portal and walked to where he was crouched, a cloak of light shimmering around her, concealing her from everyone except Wes.

"But you can close it," he said, desperately hoping he was right—that his conflict with the Queen hadn't doomed all of Vallonis. There had to be some way to stop the invasion, and he had to return to Vallonis. He'd left Nat, and who knew what was happening back there. Besides, he couldn't stand here forever, out in the open with snipers all around.

"No." The Queen shook her head.

"You can't or you won't?" Wes yelled, as the building across from them collapsed upon itself like a sand castle.

The Queen did not reply.

"You have to. Look!" he yelled, motioning to the tear in the sky, the drones and tanks that were making their way through the doorway.

She looked but did not see, her face the same immobile mask it had been since she'd appeared.

Why had she sought him? Why had she reached out to him? He hadn't trusted her from the beginning, and the doubts only grew.

Why had she appeared right then?

Because she knew he could not refuse?

Because she knew he was trapped?

Why open the portal in such a dangerous area—not to save them, surely. Nineveh did not seem to care whether he and his crew lived or died, and it was clear she despised Nat.

So why?

There was something there—something he didn't yet see, but he was beginning to grasp the edges of it, beginning to see the hand hidden in the glove, beginning to realize that all was not what it was. That perhaps he and Nat had been played like puppets in a game.

Nineveh gathered her robes.

"No," he said, putting a hand on her arm. "You're not going

anywhere." There was no getting through to her, but maybe if he brought her to the other side, she could close the portal that way. "You're coming with me," he said. Nat had tasked him to bring the Queen back to Vallonis, so he was bringing her back, whether she liked it or not.

He had already tried his power against the Queen's and triumphed. He didn't fear her. Holding her close, he rushed her back to the portal, hurrying as best he could, hoping to enter before the soldiers took notice.

He failed.

A gunshot tore through his jacket, nipping skin. Another whizzed past his ear. Someone shouted, "Stop!" but it was too late.

They were at the portal. The swirling vortex of light shimmered as he pushed through it. Already he could feel the warm sun on his hands and face, and the snow on his shoulders had nearly evaporated.

When they were through, the Queen shook off his hold. She stumbled forward, her gaze locked on the horizon. Curious, he followed behind her, wondering what had caught her eye. They were standing on a precipice overlooking the horizon. The towers of a beautiful city shimmered in the distance, shining with the glow of a thousand suns.

"What is that?" Wes asked, blinking his eyes.

"It's Apis," said Nineveh, her voice as placid as ever. "The eternal city of Vallonis. And it's burning."

11

THE FLOATING CITY OF APIS DANCED
with flames. The golden spires shimmered with sparks. Smoke twined around spindly towers, silvery arches collapsed. In the sky, winged horses flew, rescuing sylphs stranded in towers and on walls. They saved a few, but everywhere the city was crumbling. People fled atop horses, on wing or hoof; they jumped from towers or ran across the burning earth. Walls buckled, falling one on top of another, pulverizing stones, turning them to dust. The RSA had reached Apis and had done their worst. Blackened craters marred every inch of the city. Thousands cried out in pain. But the drones were merciless with their bombings, firing missiles at turrets and sending walls crumbling.

Nat had found a winged horse of her own and she urged it to fly faster. It was smaller yet more difficult to manage than her drakon, as she was unused to having to express her commands instead of executing them herself.

The sylphs flew next to her, their faces stricken.

Nat blinked back fierce tears. *Apis is burning and I never even saw the inside of it. I never even entered the city I vowed to protect.*

She had only come as far as its gates. Before one could enter Apis, one had to pass its test. Every pilgrim was made to cross a void, to take a leap of faith and believe in themselves and their power. She had stood at the cliff's edge and tried to cross the void, but had plummeted to the ground. She had failed. She had not been worthy to enter.

Was that why Nineveh called me a pretender?

Did the Queen know I had failed? Was that it?

"OVER HERE!" a voice called.

She looked down and saw Wes and Nineveh standing on the cliff at the edge of the forest. She bade her horse to land.

"Nat," said Wes, her name a sigh of relief.

She fell into his embrace, feeling restored in his presence once more. When they pulled away, she turned to Nineveh. "The portal is still open. Why?"

"What is done cannot be undone," said the Queen. "This world was never meant to be. And so at last it has met its fate."

In the distance, Apis shot off sparks, its death the collapse of a star, of all the stars. A nightmare made real. The death of a dream, its destruction ugly and sorrowful for the beauty it once held.

Now it was Nat's turn to stare at Nineveh. She exchanged a glance at Wes, who shared her frustration. She wanted to shake the Queen out of this strange paralysis that had taken hold of her. "You can stop it, but you won't. But why? If not for me, why not for them? For your people? For your world?"

Nineveh drew up her white hood over her fair hair. For a

moment her features changed, and they could see that the Queen was very, very old. She was ancient and cronelike, and the weight of the years had taken their toll. "This world is over. There is nothing that can be done."

"That's not true!" Nat cried, thinking of Faix and his dedication to teaching her how to use her power, of the task he had set before her. *Light the fire. Cast the spell. Restore the world.*

The Queen shrugged. "This world is dying; it is poisoned beyond repair. Nothing can stop its annihilation. We tried once before, sending the stolen child to the Gray Tower. But she failed. We failed. Then Faix had a dream that the protector of Vallonis had returned to us, but I did not share his belief. Did not encourage his hope." Her voice was metallic with contempt. "We became estranged because of you."

Nat was hurt and bewildered. "But why?"

"You know why."

I have seen the paths in the mirror. You will bring death to us all. Faix was the first and he will not be the last to die because of you. He died alone and away from all that he loved, because of you.

"But Faix was *bringing* me to see you," said Nat. "I stood at the gates of Apis."

"As a last, quixotic idea. You see, he hoped to change my mind. But as you discovered, you were not worthy to enter Apis, were you?" said the Queen, the frost in her voice as cold as a bitter winter chill.

Nat remembered standing at the ledge, staring at Apis, fashioning an image that would be made real; she had made something out of nothing, shaped a bridge that would lead her to the other side. She had done it. She knew she had. And yet she had fallen anyway. She stared at the Queen and suddenly she knew why she had failed.

"I didn't fail. I made that bridge. You kept me out," said Nat. "It was you."

Nat saw it all now. The Queen did not believe in Faix. The Queen did not believe Vallonis had a protector. The Queen did not lift a finger to defend the city or close the portal. The Queen had stood and watched while Vallonis was destroyed and Apis fell from the sky.

Nineveh was no friend.

She was as much an enemy as the RSA battalions that charged into the peaceful valley. *Nothing can stop its annihilation*, Nineveh had said, and so instead of hampering it, she had hastened it.

Wes had cautioned Nat to wait and warned her that he didn't trust Nineveh. He had wanted to find another way out, but Nat had been so blind. She had begged him to trust her.

She felt faint, unsteady, even as Nineveh continued to regard her with that calm, icy gaze. Wes slung an arm around her shoulder, and only then did Nat realize that she was trembling.

Because it all snapped into place, and she knew Wes knew, too. He must have figured it out, when Nineveh wouldn't close the portal from the other side. And he had brought her here anyway, because Nat had asked him to.

"You did this," Nat gasped, feeling her knees weaken at the thought and glad that she had Wes to lean on. "You knew Wes would break the seal on the portal if you threatened to keep me out. *You knew what would happen.* You used your power to find him and you *used* him to break it. You used him. You used *us*." With horror, she realized Nineveh had used Wes's love for her to bring about this chaos. Used it like a weapon.

No, Nineveh hadn't come to New Kandy to save them. She had come to New Kandy because the army was there.

They had only been pawns in a game, played like cards thrown on the felt and discarded on the flop.

"You wanted Vallonis destroyed all along, you *wanted* this to happen. You made it happen!" cried Nat. "But why?"

"What is done cannot be undone. As I've said before, this world was never meant to be," she repeated forcefully, anger breaking through her cool marble façade. "The promise of Atlantis is over. The dream of Avalon dies here. It dies with me. There is no magic that can stop what has begun now. This is the end. There is no hope for Vallonis, for anyone left in the world, gray or blue."

"There won't be anyone left thanks to you," muttered Wes.

Nineveh ignored him and raised her arms. "I was here in the beginning when we cast the spell the first time. And the second. And the third will be the last. There will be none other." There was a huge flash of brilliant white, and then the Queen disappeared—or more like disintegrated in front of their eyes.

"Good riddance," said Wes.

Nat stared at the empty space where the Queen had stood. Her anger and guilt made her stomach turn, but Wes's solid weight next to her was a comfort, a bulwark against the pain in her soul.

"It was her, Nat, she did this," he said. "Not us."

Yes, but . . .

Our love doomed this world.

No matter what, we played a part in its destruction.

And the thought was a sliver, the beginning of the wedge that would grow between them, one so small she couldn't even see it right at the moment.

But it was there.

More soldiers poured through the portal, more drones, an army of invaders. Their iron-toed boots pounded the forest floor; their machines and rocket fire made the air vibrate. There was no stopping their conquest. They would murder the people and ravish the land, claiming as their own whatever resources they had not destroyed.

She'd lost her drakon, the portal was open, Apis was burning. The Queen had abandoned them. But Wes was right, of course. And it wasn't over. Not while they were still standing. Nat was the protector of Vallonis. Or was she just kidding herself? Was there anything left *to protect*?

A terrible noise—a great crack as if the earth itself were breaking open—interrupted her thoughts. Nat's eyes widened, her mouth agape in fear. Wes held her. Apis was no longer just burning; it was faltering, crashing to the earth. With a sound that dwarfed a thousand thunderclaps, the great capital of Vallonis fell from the heavens, struck the ground, and shattered. A tremor buckled the earth beneath them. The cliffs behind them trembled, trees quivered. The very earth shuddered. The city was destroyed. Apis was gone.

In the hazy distance, men and women poured out from

the city's ruins. Like ants fleeing the hive, they hurried in long lines, searching for a means of escape from the burning metropolis. Apis was at their backs, and to the side were mountains, cliffs too steep to traverse. They had only one way to go, and the soldiers were blocking it, shooting down anyone who came their way.

The winged cavalry charged, and as the white-haired general dashed into battle, the drones surrounded him, circling him, showering him with rocket fire. He raised his sword and sent a wave of thunder and lightning their way. There was a scream and a crash as everything fell to the ground.

Yet when the haze dissipated, there was no one left standing, foes and friends alike. There was only a pile of bodies, soldiers and sylphs, the general on top, his eyes lifeless, skin the color of gray concrete.

"Father!" Liannan cried, swooping down from the sky, landing and leaving her winged horse and rushing to his side, Shakes right behind her. The sound of her grief was terrible to hear.

The tanks rumbled their way, and the soldiers began shooting at their friends. Soon, all of Vallonis would fall to their hands.

"Get everyone together," Nat told Wes. "Tell them to flee, to run as far away from the army as possible. And as far away from me."

"What are you going to do?" he asked fearfully, worried for her as always.

"I'm going to burn," Nat said softly. She had to call up the drakonfire somehow. She had to use her power to stop this, it was the only way. "But without my drakon I don't know if I can control it." She couldn't help but shiver at the thought of the wildfire raging across the plains of the Blue.

"Hold on," said Wes. "Before you set yourself on fire, I have an idea." He turned to Shakes. "Get everyone away!" he ordered. "Get as far from us as you can!"

Shakes nodded and, with the help of their remaining crew, began to steer the dazed and the dying to the other side of the field.

Nat looked deep into Wes's kind brown eyes. She had found love there, compassion, and partnership. Whatever she had to do, she would do it with him at her side.

"Do you trust me?" he asked.

"Always," she promised. She took his hand in hers. "But I don't want to hurt you."

"You won't," he said staunchly. "I can resist magic, remember? I'm a living antidote. How's that for talent?" He tightened his grip. "Go on. Do what you have to do. I will burn with you."

Nat closed her eyes, seeking the flame within her soul. Drakonfire. The white flame. She searched for the feeling she had when she was bonded to Mainas. She tried to recall that sensation, the heat of the drakonflame, what it felt like to be united with her mount. It hadn't been that long since their separation, but she struggled to recall that emotion, that heat.

She was the drakon, its fire and its fury.

She tried to block out the sounds of the battle, the cries

of the sylphs trampled beneath the soldiers, the exploding rockets. Each moment she delayed, another life passed from this world, another bit of beauty died at the barrel of a gun, crushed underneath the wheels of a tank.

She reached deep into herself, deep into her heart.

Where is it? Where is my strength, where is my fury? I am the drakon's wild heart. I am the drakon's unfettered soul. Where is the fire that is within me?

Why, I gave it to Wes, she remembered now. She had put her soul into his. She had sent the white spark into his body to restart his heart.

He carried the flame within him, so all she had to do was reach for it and take it back.

She felt his hand in hers and squeezed it tightly. *Come back to me,* she whispered to the drakonfire.

Just like that, when she opened her eyes she saw there was a white flame dancing between their clasped hands. Wes smiled.

Nat waved her hand and the flame grew, trailing her fingers like a white, shimmering streamer. She waved it in a circle and the flames danced around them, the two of them in the center of a glistening circle of fire. She waved her hand in another circle, then another. Her fingers drew flames in the air, she was painting with fire. Again and again the flames circled them growing ever more dense.

Wes stood in the center with her, watching, waiting.

She could no longer see the individual streams; there was nothing but a tornado of fire swirling around them.

It felt good, like the heart of the drakon. The flame comforted her like an old friend; she rediscovered that part of her soul that she so desperately missed.

She was the drakon.

Its heart of dread.

And now she was an immense, churning, howling ball of flame.

12

WES STOOD IN THE CENTER OF THE FIRE, holding back the heat from the flame. It danced around them, wild and furious, but when he held out his hands it flickered and stilled. *You will not burn us. You will not devour her,* he said to the flame. *I know you. You have burned inside me. I am part of you now.*

"Let's do this," he said to Nat, cocking his head toward the battlefield. "Together."

Nat nodded and reached her arms out to the sky so that the white flames shot up in the air. Wes sculpted the drakonfire into mighty columns, and Nat sent them hurtling across the battlefield, forcing the soldiers away from the people who were still coming out of the city. She sent the soldiers running back to the portal, back to New Kandy and the gray world where they belonged. Her fire shot up through the clouds, incinerating a column of drones.

Walking in the protective circle of drakonfire, the two of them made their way across the battlefield to rescue the refugees of Apis. The citizens of the once-fair city were fighting back, turning guns into smoke, showering the soldiers with hail made of boulders, setting fire to their vehicles, their tanks, and their drones. Their general had been felled, but there was someone else leading them now.

It was Liannan, holding up a bow and arrow and letting the arrows take flight, Shakes astride behind her, brandishing a stolen automatic rifle. The rest of the crew followed, shooting back at those who aimed at the beautiful golden-haired sylph.

Liannan's silver arrows cut through a line of soldiers. Her people fought well, using magic against bullets, weaving illusions, making the soldiers fire at places where no one stood, making them attack one another or their drones. They filled the sky with illusory smoke, with clouds shaped like a drakon, with swirls of brightly colored mist, confusing tanks and their automatic sighting systems.

But even magic had limits. They could distract the soldiers, fool them sometimes, but when it came to ground combat, they were badly outgunned and outnumbered. Soldiers hacked at the smallmen and showered the sylphs with gunfire.

Vallonis was losing.

Wes focused on holding and controlling Nat's drakonfire. Like lava flows, the fire cut through the battalions, separating them from the sylphs and the city they were abandoning. He marveled at how well they worked together. It was as if they had one power, one strength, that they both wielded.

But it wasn't enough. It would not be enough to forge victory from defeat.

The sylphs were easily mowed down by automatic weaponry. Their feared heartrenders could not stop the tanks from rolling over everything in their path. Whole families fell dead on the grassy plain, and more would join them if the assault continued much longer.

Wes caught Nat's eye.

"I need to burn," she said, her voice hollow. "Go. Shield them from the fire. Protect them from me."

Wes did not argue. He knew what had to be done. She didn't have to ask because he already knew. He was holding her back, he knew, limiting her power.

There was no other way out of this battle than to let her burn.

13

SHE WATCHED AS HE RAN TO THE remaining sylphs and their loyal crew. "Retreat! Retreat!" Wes yelled, throwing up a shield around them as they ran away.

Nat stood stock-still as the flames grew taller and wilder around her. The white fire was stronger now—hotter, but she felt no warmth. Instead, a current of electricity ran through her body; she was alive, awake, energetic. Without Wes to hold it back, the ball of flame was now a hurricane of fire, a tower that stretched up and out over the bloody fields and into the drone-filled sky. It leapt up into the clouds, turning them to mist. It billowed still higher, shedding a light as pure as starlight, illuminating the field of battle. A wondrous, fearsome sight. The light shone upon the faces of the soldiers, making their pale faces turn a shade whiter. They looked like ghosts, their mouths gaping, eyes staring in wonder.

Protect them from me, she had told Wes as the hurricane became an even greater storm, a tempest beyond imagining. She watched as the survivors hurried to Wes's side, as he stood in the middle of the crowd, eyes closed, focusing on his magic. The shield he crafted was invisible, a glass dome like the one that shielded the El Dorado. It sparkled when the flames touched it. He would keep them safe. His power was everything that hers was not. It was safety, protection. It was silent and invisible, quiet like the man who wielded it. His magic could do no harm. For the span of a heartbeat, she wished that was her talent as well, but Nat had a different lot in life.

When the last survivor was safe beneath the shield, she let out the rest of her flame. She opened up her every pore, unleashing all the power within her. She half expected the soldiers to run, to flee back through the portal, but the men would not stand down. They faced her flame with rocket fire, an endless barrage of bullets. Gunshots tore through the great inferno, but none reached Nat. The flames consumed all of it. The heat melted their ammunition, crumpled their tanks. It scorched the earth itself, turning trees into glowing toothpicks, burning down the trunks, incinerating the roots, leaving only holes in the earth. Her fire twisted through the armies of the RSA, leaving heaps of molten metal, clouds of smoke.

Only Wes stood against the flame. His power kept the people of Apis safe as the fire rippled across the battlefield. The transparent shield glowed yellow and orange reflecting the flames. Nat caught glimpses of the people huddled together inside. As the next wave hit the dome, it sparkled again, turning gold. But the next blast tore the shield and a cascade of flame poured into the dome. Screams echoed against the roar, her tempest.

No! she cried, dampening the fire until the hurricane of flame subsided as Wes worked to close the hole.

That was when the bullet struck her, as the soldiers took advantage of her moment of weakness. The bullet tore through the flesh of her upper arm. The flames rose once more around her, as a second bullet whizzed past her ear, and something exploded nearby. The sound was deafening.

I need to finish this. Nat drew the flames around her, letting their heat build, stoking the great fire, the ever-expanding storm. While her fire built up again, the army changed tactics. They gave up fighting Nat and trained all of their guns of the people of Vallonis. Every bit of their firepower was aimed at Wes's shield. The shield had turned from gold to brown to black, and the dome was flexing, like a bubble about to pop.

The people within crowded together, their eyes on the flames and collapsing dome. Wes strained as he held the shield. Peering through the flames, Nat caught his gaze. The grim set of his mouth told her she had to do it, to give it every last bit that she had. He would hold the line. He would not let the shield collapse; nothing would come through. His strength matched her own.

Confident in his power, that he would keep them safe from her, Nat called up the biggest fireball she could create. The field became a churning ocean of fire, a roiling sea of death. Its white tongue danced over and consumed every surface, turning the field and everything and everyone on it into dust. The fire sparked the connection between her and Mainas once more. In the fire, she was one with her drakon, and so she let it rage as long as she could, until every last bit of her power was spent. She was a wound, a gash, and now her life was bleeding out. She'd given it all to the flame.

Just like that, it was over. There was nothing left. Everything was ash.

Nat dropped to her knees.

14

WHEN THE FIRE RETREATED, WES LET down his shield, falling to the ground, dizzy and sick from the effort. The heat had been immense, a great weight he had pushed back against, holding the firestorm at bay. His heart was pounding painfully in his chest. Just like the death races back in New Vegas, it brought that same rush of adrenaline.

He had seen and felt and stood in the center of the fierce and terrible heart of the drakon, the angry thing that burned within Nat. *I understand her now, the weight she carries, the danger.* He had tested his strength against hers and had survived.

Barely. But he had survived nonetheless.

Wes turned to his crew. "Everyone all right?" he asked, looking to Liannan, Shakes, the smallmen and what was left of the sylphs of Apis. They were rubbing the red from their eyes, trying to recover from the heat and the flame. All that remained of Wes's luminous shield was a circle of green grass, a relic of the once-beautiful field. The grass and flowers were trampled in places and dotted with blood.

His own throat was dry as sandpaper, his eyes blurry from tears, working to overcompensate against the heat, but he had no thought to his own health or safety. He scanned the burnt field for Nat, calling her name over and over until his voice was hoarse.

He'd caught glimpses of her during the firestorm, her slender figure outlined by fire. He thought he'd found her gaze when the dome faltered, but he'd lost track of her in the final deluge. The world had gone white for a moment—he'd seen only light.

When it faded there was nothing left of the army, its soldiers, drones, or tanks. There was nothing left of anything. Nat had burned it all.

"Nat!" he called, stumbling through the ashy field, trying not to knock into the still-smoking heaps of metal, the hills of molten steel and rubber that had once been tanks or drones. Smoke was everywhere, spouting from holes in the ground and the edges of the forest. The flames had left nothing untouched. The flat field was now marred by pits, craters the size of cars dotting the landscape. He might as well have been standing on the moon. The land was so blasted and barren, he almost forgot that this had once been paradise, that just moments before there had been grass here and trees.

"Wes!"

He heard his name. It shot through the smoke, mixing with the sound of crackling embers, the soft echoes of his footfalls on the ash.

"Nat!" he called through the mist. The stench of burnt

metal made him cough. There was movement among the ruins, something trembling in the distance. He nearly fell into a pit, almost stepped on glowing embers.

He found her in the middle of the dust and ash. She was crouched like a child, her knees to her chin, her arms wrapped around herself, hugging her tight. Her hair and her armor were as black as the field around her, and when he said her name gently, she did not respond.

"Nat." He crouched next to her, and when he put a hand on her shoulder he almost pulled it away—it was hot to the touch, like an open flame. But he kept his hand where it was. "Nat, you did it. You stopped them," he said.

Finally she looked up to meet his eyes and the pain in hers made his stomach turn.

"What did I stop?" she whispered, not seeing him, motioning to the burnt field, the dark sky, the smoking ruins of Apis.

He knew what she meant; he'd grown up hearing tales of the mythical Blue, the land without ice, a place of warmth and beauty. Now it just looked like the rest of the world: ruined; toxic; a smoky, charred wasteland. The apocalypse had come to Vallonis. Everything around them was black, destroyed, burnt.

"What kind of victory is this? What did we win?" she asked, her eyes dark hollows in her pale face.

"It doesn't matter. You stopped the army. We survived," said Wes. "You saved everyone."

"I saved Vallonis only to destroy it." She hung her head in her arms, and her shoulders shook in a silent cry.

"They will rebuild and recover, when you cast the spell, when you make the world anew," he said, wanting to comfort her.

His hand burned from where he had touched her, and Nat did not reply; her eyes were glazed and her mouth slack. Wes began to worry. Had the fire burned her out from the inside?

"Nat, come on," he said gently. "Stand up."

She closed her eyes and exhaled. "Mainas has returned to me," she said softly. "I can see with the drakonsight again. When I called up the flame, I got it back."

Wes leaned closer, knowing this was important, knowing he had to help her reclaim the bond. "What did you see?"

"A ruined city, covered in ice, near the water." She squinted and her forehead crumpled in the effort.

"What else? Any landmarks? Any clue as to where they are?" he pressed. "Keep trying."

"Hard to remember . . . but I think . . . I think I saw a fallen statue on the water. An enormous one." She shook her head. "Of a woman holding a torch."

"Liberty," said Wes. "Eliza must be in New Dead City." What was once called New York, now lost to the ice, covered in darkness and eternal winter.

Nat's eyes remained closed. "There are jeeps, tanks, tracking them across the mainland, but they are days away yet."

Suddenly, her eyes flew open. "I need to find them!" she said, almost panicked. "While I still have the drakonsight!" She trembled, exhausted and fragile from the effort as well as the aftereffects of the battle.

Wes caught her as she stumbled, pulled held her toward

him, let her fall against him, shaking and scared. "Mainas needs you to rest," he said. "And heal. We all do. There is time yet—Avo is hampered by the ocean and the refuse, and there are a million ways to hide in New Dead City; it will take some time to find them even with the drones."

"I don't need to rest," she said. "I need to find them. I need to get my drakon back!"

"You can't win against her in your state," he argued. "If you go now, you will only put yourself in more danger." He saw the blood brimming in the corners of her eyes, the way her hands shook like leaves in the wind, the way her eyes did not focus, did not see him.

Nat pulled away, seized with panic. "No! You can't stop me! I won't let you! Let me go!" Her eyes were crazed, wild with raw animal fear. "GET AWAY FROM ME!"

"What are you doing? Nat!" He reached for her, and she screamed.

"Don't! Don't touch me!" she shrieked. "GET AWAY!" She scrabbled away from him, kicking up dust in his face as she stood up. She was a sight to behold, her bright eyes glittering in her ash-covered face.

Wes followed her, keeping his voice calm. He knew it was the drakonblood speaking, the monster inside her that spoke to him this way. This wasn't Nat. His Nat.

"Nat—it's me," he said, pleading.

"Don't take another step closer!" Her voice was low and threatening.

Unafraid, he stepped forward. Another step. "I'm not

stopping you from going after them. I just want you to rest until you're whole and healed."

The fire in her eyes flickered and she held up her hand against him, a fireball dancing in front of the palm on her hand. "One more step and I will burn you to the ground," she whispered.

And for a moment he did fear her, but he took another step closer. "It's me. Ryan," he said, using the name no one used but his family and Nat, for Nat was his family now. He opened his arms wide as he looked deep into her eyes, addressing the raging fire within. "You're not going to hurt me, Nat. I'm not afraid of you."

The fire trembled in her palm, flickering and bright. She raised her hand, ready to scorch him as she had the armies of invaders.

Wes braced himself for the blast, unwilling to leave her side. But the fire never came. He opened his eyes to see Nat falling to her knees, sobbing.

"Yes," she cried. "Ryan, it's you."

He took her in his arms again, held her close. She was still warm, but no longer burning.

"I was going to hurt you," she said.

"Never, you would never do that," he replied, willing it to be true, even if the memory of fear and doubt was so clear.

"What happened?" she asked, looking around at the blackened field as if for the first time, at the piles of ash that were all that remained of the battle that had raged on the plain.

"We won," he said. "They're gone. Your drakonfire closed

the portal to our world as well." They looked up to the sky, which was whole and no longer torn.

"Mainas . . . ," she whispered. "I felt him. I saw them."

"We will find your drakon and get it back from Eliza," he said. "I made a vow to you and yours. Mainas is part of you. You will be whole."

She nodded, and the tears fell freely now as she surveyed the devastated landscape. He knew she was crying because Apis was destroyed and Vallonis burnt, but she was also mourning the lives she had taken, every soul a mark on hers.

"I am a monster," she whispered.

He shook his head. "No. I don't believe that and neither should you."

"I will doom everyone around me," she said, in a voice so low that he strained to hear it. "I will bring death to all I love. The Queen told me I would."

"Nat, Nat, Nat," he said, running his hands up and down her arms, as if he were trying to calm her down or put out the fire, even though she was no longer burning. But what he was feeling was too hard to put into words, so he just held her close, saying her name over and over again, letting her lean against him, so that she fit under his chin, her heart against his. Holding her so tightly as if his love could anchor her to the ground, could hold the drakonfire at bay. His strength had shielded the survivors against her fire, but he had not been able to shield her from herself.

It felt as if they had been holding on to each other for hours when Liannan came up to them. Wes released Nat gently.

She nodded to let him know she was okay. They turned to their friend. The sylph's silver armor was streaked with blood, grease, and dust. Her face was grave. "We need you," she said to them. "We're getting everyone to follow us to Alfarhome, to my village."

"I need to go to New Dead City. Mainas is there," said Nat. "My drakonsight returned, and I must follow while I can."

"Yes, but first you must rest," said Wes. "Let the fire left within you burn out. You need to get your bearings back before we can go anywhere."

Liannan nodded. "Nat, Wes is right. We all need rest, especially you. And you can't fight Eliza without a drakon of your own."

"Then I won't stand a chance, as Mainas was the last," said Nat.

"The last of his time," said Liannan.

Nat was startled by her words. "What are you saying?"

But before the sylph could explain, Brendon found them. "Liannan," he said, his voice panicked and high. "Come. It's Roark."

THE RED AND THE BLACK

Red, the color of desire
Black, the color of despair
—"RED AND BLACK," *LES MISÉRABLES*

15

FAIX. FAROUK. ROARK.

Nat stood at the edge of the circle, watching as Shakes and Wes gently lowered the smallman's coffin into the ground. They were gathered in the graveyard in Liannan's village a few days after the battle. Brendon laid the first rose upon Roark's grave, his eyes red and dry, the depths of his sadness beyond mere tears and sobbing. Nat understood. She, too, was numb, crippled, spent.

The peaceful vista of Liannan's homestead brought little comfort, even though they had spent a restful few days convalescing in the serene village nestled at the foot of the White Mountains. In the shadow of the tall cliffs, slender houses sheltered beneath spindly white trees. Their branches cast spotted shadows on the sun-drenched dwellings, and at sunset the village glowed with a radiant purple light. Everything was alive here and everything held magic. Even the leaves seemed to have a mind of their own; they would swirl in great whirlwinds, drifting through the air as if they were putting on a show, entertaining any who watched. Lavender carpeted the earth, releasing a scent so sweet it made eyes water, and the purple blossoms unfurled whenever Nat approached, welcoming her into their presence. The houses themselves were plain in construction, but made from a pale wood that had the appearance of ivory, white as chalk and hard as steel.

While Nat was consoled by the fact that there were some places of Vallonis that survived the RSA invasion, it was hard to discount the devastation the battle had wrought.

In the far distance, Apis lay in ruins. Three of her friends were dead, along with Liannan's father, the many sylphs and smallmen of Vallonis, the countless lives she took on the field when she burned the RSA army. They were just soldiers following orders. Many of them younger than she was. They had died screaming, melting into the flame.

You will bring death to everyone around you.

The fire within her had finally died, but she still remembered how close she had been to hurting Wes. She had held the flame in her hand, ready to reduce him to ashes.

You will destroy him.

What was she doing? What was she protecting? What was her purpose? Once, she had believed she was a warrior, a guardian. The one who was promised, foretold. But she was beginning to worry that the Queen knew better, that Nat was a danger rather than a savior to the people around her.

Wes joined her side to hear Liannan's blessing. He had dark circles under his eyes, dirt on his hands, and the grief he felt lay heavy on his shoulders, but when he saw her, his smile was as sweet as the late summer wind that blew over the cornflowers.

I will not destroy him. He will be safe from me, always. It was a promise to herself that she swore she would die keeping.

After the burial, Nat sought Liannan's attention. She had tried to find time to speak to her friend privately before, but it had been difficult as the sylph had many responsibilities that fell on her shoulders now that her father was dead and the Queen had disappeared. Nat found her in her father's library, perusing his books.

Like everything in the village, every shelf and wall in the library was made of the same white wood from the nearby forest, polished to a grain so fine it looked as if it glowed from within. While plain in design and furnishings, it was a place of great beauty in its perfect and natural simplicity. The books it contained were not bound in leather or any animal hide; instead the manuscripts were deckle-edged and held together with flaxen thread. The text was inked in a careful and flowing script, the pages made from a buttery yellow paper.

When Liannan saw Nat, she put down the volume she was holding. "I'm sorry, I know you've been trying to find me."

Nat closed the door behind her and nodded. "And you have been avoiding me."

"I didn't want to address it until you were healed," Liannan said. "I didn't want you running off before you were ready."

"I guessed as much. You and Wes, conspiring against me," Nat joked weakly. It felt like blasphemy to laugh on such a hard day, when they had just buried their friend. Kind and dear Roark, who always had a smile and an unexpected treat in his pockets, who would share the last of his rations with anyone who needed it, who had given his life so that others could live.

But mourning was a luxury she could not afford at the moment. She held the grief at bay and cleared her throat. "You hinted that Mainas is not the only drakon in the world."

"Yes."

"But it can't be. They're all dead, all but mine. Faix said as much."

Liannan nodded slowly and pulled the white robe around her delicate shoulders as she leaned against the marble-topped table. "There is only one drakon in *this* world. But the drakon you seek is not *in* this world. There is another. The one that belonged to Faix."

Nat tried to recall what Faix had told her about his drakon. He'd said it was gone from this world. She'd thought he meant it was dead. "So if it's not dead, where is it?" she asked.

"In the Great Conservatory of Apis, there is a door that leads to the Red Lands, the remains of all that was once Atlantis and Avalon. And those ruins are guarded by a drakon. Faix's drakon. When the ice came, and the corruption, it is said that Faix sent it there for its own safety. The door is shut with his mark." She let her words settle while Nat absorbed the information. "Only the drakonrydder can open the door. If you want a drakon, you can bring it back here to fight for your own."

"And how do I convince it to follow me?"

"You are the last drakonrydder of Vallonis, the one who was promised," said Liannan. "You will prove yourself true."

Nat brooded over that complication. She would have to bond with a new drakon, one that had been alone for over a century. Who knew what state the creature was in, whether it was even still sane?

"I don't envy your task," said Liannan sadly, leaning back in her father's chair.

The two friends were quiet for a long moment. Nat looked at the row of shelves, marveling at the wealth of wisdom contained in one small library. She broke the silence, wanting to unburden herself a little on her friend. "If I succeed, do you know what will be asked of me, when I cast the Archimedes spell?" she asked, walking toward the window so that Liannan would not see the fear in her face.

Liannan nodded. "All of Vallonis knows. Magic demands sacrifice, as do all acts of creation. And the birthing of the new world will require the greatest sacrifice of all. This is the way of our people, of magic itself."

Sacrifice. Nat stood at the window, looking to where Brendon was still standing by Roark's grave. "Is there no other way?"

"No," said Liannan sadly.

Nat understood the tenets of sacrifice. She had risked her life every day for Vallonis and had not once asked for a single favor in return. She'd had no thought for gratitude or comfort. She'd been a good soldier. The only reward she needed was to be left alone at the end of it all, to be free to have a peaceful life with Wes somewhere.

But the sacrifice demanded of the spell meant there would be no peace, no future for them. It meant death. The loss of everyone she loved. She would be alone at the end of the story, at the end of her journey.

"There is no hope then. No hope at all?" she asked, with a catch in her throat.

Liannan's voice was kind. "Nat, my friend, there is always hope."

A knock on the library door interrupted their conversation.

"There you are," Wes said, his handsome face appearing in the doorway, looking relieved to have found her. For the past few days, he had hardly left her side, reading to her while she rested, watching over her while she slept. When the fever turned, she had woken up in a sweat and found him draped over a chair next to her, enduring the uncomfortable position so they would not be parted.

For the past few days they had read books together, taken long walks through the mountain trails, their hands entwined. Now she nodded but did not smile at him, or go to his side as she usually did.

Nat avoided his eyes, as Nineveh's words echoed in her ear once more. Her new dark mantra. *You will bring death to everyone around you, death to all whom you love. You will destroy him.* Somehow, she had to make sure that didn't happen.

She had to save them all from sharing her fate. Especially Wes. But how? Then she realized the answer was so simple.

She would push him away, as far away from her as possible, to keep him alive. It was the only way to make certain that he would not be destroyed, that he would not share her fate, her sacrifice.

It was the only way to ensure his survival. Her determination renewed her energy, and when Wes came to stand next

124

to her, she flinched from his touch, from the arm he circled around her waist.

He shot her a curious look. "What's going on?"

Nat hesitated, but Liannan answered and seemed to decide for her. "I told Nat where to find another drakon."

"Where?" He raised his eyebrows. That was Wes, always straight to the point, asking no unnecessary questions about how Liannan came upon this surprising news.

Liannan explained the intricacies of breaching the hidden universe. She handed Wes a parchment. "This is a map of Apis. You will need to sort through the rubble to find the place where the conservatory once stood. There you will find what you seek."

Wes pocketed the map. "We'll leave as soon as it's safe to," he said to Nat.

"You don't have to come with me," she said.

"I don't have to, I want to." It was clear there was no arguing him out of it, and while Nat worried this would only make things harder later on, she was glad to have a little more time with him yet.

"And once we're in, how do we get out? Through the same door?" asked Wes sharply, already strategizing their journey.

Liannan shook her head.

"Of course not, nothing's ever that simple, is it?" He folded his arms across his chest, his piercing eyes trained on Nat, and she knew he was still wondering why she had rebuffed him earlier.

She remained rooted at the spot, determined to keep her distance. She turned her attention back to Liannan.

"It is said that once the red drakon leaves the Red Lands, the hidden universe will collapse, and you will be returned to the conservatory of Apis. Fail to remove him, and you will remain forever in the Red Lands."

"Got it," said Wes. "Tame the beast and get the hell out, or stay and rot."

Liannan removed a stone from a jar on one of the shelves and handed it to Wes. It was pure white, almost translucent.

"What's this?" he asked, as it gleamed in his palm.

"A speaking stone. It will grant you a bit of sylph power, the ability to communicate to us in your thoughts. We will use it to advise each other of our location once you are out of the red."

"Got it. Magic cell phone." He winked and shoved it into his coat.

Nat had to smile at that.

"So if that's all, I was going to check on the rest of the team," he said.

"There is something else," said Liannan. "They say the ruined world is dangerous, that it is haunted by the dead. Be wary."

"No problem." Wes shrugged. "I'm sure we've taken on worse."

"Nevertheless a warrior needs a weapon," said Liannan, reaching for a black sword that hung on the wall.

"I'd prefer a rifle if you've got one," he said.

Liannan ignored his comment as she offered it to Nat, and Wes looked abashed. But Liannan did not seem to notice. "It was my father's. It is made of drakonbone. He believed in the protector of Vallonis, in the Resurrection of the Flame, in the spell that would make the world anew. Use it well," she said, handing Nat the weapon.

Nat bowed as she took the sword, and caught Wes's eye. He was like a little boy, sometimes, wanting to play with the new toy. She felt a rush of affection for him, accompanied by another wave of sadness. *He deserves more than I can give him.*

"Can I?" he asked.

"Be my guest."

She studied his face, his hands as he grasped the sword hilt, loving even the way his fingers crooked over the blade.

While Wes admired the blade, Nat turned to the window again, looking out in the distance, at the smoldering ruins of Apis. She had once pictured herself returning to the city as a hero, a valiant protector, welcomed within its gates. She had pictured a grand triumph, a celebration of her victory over the drone fleet. Now she would return as a thief, picking through the rubble to plunder the last traces of the city's magic.

"While you claim the red drakon, we will take those who can still fight and look for Eliza in New Dead City. If the RSA does not stop her from getting to the Gray Tower, we will," Liannan told them. "Shakes and Brendon already know and have agreed to accompany me."

A handful of sylphs and smallmen, Shakes, Liannan, and Brendon, Nat counted. Against the most powerful sorceress the world had seen. Eliza had stolen almost every marked person's power for herself, rendering her practically invincible. The odds were horrifying, and she wasn't alone in her calculation.

"That's a suicide mission," said Wes. "Wait until we return, and we'll all go."

"We cannot take that risk. Eliza must not reach the Gray Tower before Nat does," said Liannan.

"Give us a week."

"We don't have a week. By Shakes's guess, we are behind a few days already."

Liannan was right, Nat knew. The longer they stalled, the greater the risk that everything would be destroyed. They would have to gamble with their lives.

"We'll get there as soon as we can," said Wes. "With a drakon and a magic cell phone how can we lose?"

The girls had to smile at that.

"Now if you don't mind, I need to tell Shakes to get our supplies prepared." Liannan said her good-bye and left the two of them in the room alone.

"Hey, stranger," he said, teasing her for her aloofness. "You ready for this?"

She shrugged and turned away abruptly, heading for the door and brushing by him without returning his smile. "I'm sorry . . . I forgot I have to ask Liannan about one last thing."

Nat saw his face fall and knew she had hurt him with her dismissiveness, but it was nothing compared to keeping him alive. To keeping him safe, safe from the dark fate that hung over her, like a guillotine blade, ready to sever her heart.

She had made her choice. She would push him away.

She would save his life by breaking his heart, shattering her own in the process.

She would travel to the ruins of the old world.

And leave with a drakon to fight her own.

128

16

AT LAST THE DAY THAT WES HAD DREADED finally arrived—the day he would be separated from his crew. It felt as if there were a doomsday clock ticking away his fate by the second, and now it was chiming. He didn't very much like the idea of splitting up the team—it felt like a bad move, that their resources would be limited, stretched thin to breaking.

If he and Nat failed, they would be trapped in some funky alternative universe with an angry drakon. Meanwhile Shakes, Liannan, and Brendon and what was left of the warriors of Vallonis were heading to New Dead City, to stop Eliza, who was insane, not to mention armed to the teeth with mega-magic and Nat's drakon, in a region crawling with the other half of the RSA force and Avo Hubik searching for the same thing they were. Wes didn't know which was worse.

He was worried for his friends. Yet he was worried about Nat more. At first he'd chalked it up to battle fatigue, and the lingering effects of the drakonfire that had raged within her. But ever since Liannan had told them about the red drakon,

Nat hadn't been herself. She was short with him, indifferent and preoccupied. They'd hardly spent any time alone together.

Did he do something wrong? If so, what could it have been? He'd been racking his brains but couldn't come up with anything. Had he misunderstood something in some way? Why didn't she want him around all of a sudden?

He'd even gotten the distinct feeling that she only let him accompany her to Apis because Liannan had insisted on it. Nat had tried to sell the idea of heading into the Red Lands alone, but no one was buying it.

And now it was as if she was avoiding him on purpose. Whenever he asked her what was wrong, or if there was any way he could help, she shook him off, as if he were a pest.

Speaking of shaking, he couldn't shake the notion that the Nat who had won the battle for them, the one who had emerged from the ashes like a broken bird, was someone else. More and more he was beginning to believe that the fire she had called up that day had indeed burned her inside out, and had left a hollow, brittle shell of a person where his girl used to be.

Because *his* Nat, the one who had saved him from death, the one who had kissed him on the deck of the ship, never cringed when he touched her, nor did she ever once act as if his very presence were painful to her.

That's what it felt like, that it was *painful* for her to be around him. It was getting to him, and so the only thing he could think of was that she was not herself. Not his Nat anymore.

Because *this* Nat, this post-battle Nat, was all business.

Wes wanted to tell her that he, too, was broken and grieving and tired and sad. But one look at her stony, angry face and the words died on his lips, and so they had said nothing of any meaning to each other in the days leading up to their departure.

It was killing him, but he didn't show it, keeping his poker face.

He desperately wanted his Nat back, but he didn't know how you could make someone be the person you wanted them to be when they didn't seem to have any interest in being that person anymore.

At dawn that morning, Wes found Shakes standing outside the house, whose white walls reflected the bright sun, making everything sparkle. His friend was standing by the woodpile and smoking one of those fragrant violet cigarettes the sylphs favored, a pensive look on his face. They had both traded in their burnt and bloodied uniforms for what they jokingly called sylph wear—handsome forest-green garments edged with leather patches and trim. In truth, it didn't look that much different from the camouflage they were used to wearing, except this was green instead of white.

"Smoke?" Shakes asked, holding out the pack kept neatly in a wooden box.

Wes declined.

"So," said Shakes, who always spoke first when he was nervous. "You guys really going into some other world to fetch another drakon?"

"Guess so."

"Yeah." Shakes looked around him, at the soft fields of lavender, thyme, and rosemary, their colors intensified by the morning sun. Birds circled the tall gray cliffs and the leaves danced in the air; even the flowers seemed to bend and sway at his ankles. "Check it out, you and me in the Blue. Never thought it would happen. Too bad it's all ending."

"You believe all that stuff now? About the tower and the spell?" asked Wes. "I thought you were a skeptic."

"Not anymore," said Shakes, exhaling slowly. "Don't you feel it? Like we're all on the edge of something? And everything could end at any moment? This isn't going to last. It can't."

Wes thought it over. "Nat says the world is dying, it's poisoned, and if she doesn't cast the spell, it's all over."

"Yup. I believe her." Shakes stomped out his cigarette. He lifted his chin, nodded to Wes. "You take care, boss," he said, offering his fist.

Wes pounded it. "You, too, man."

They had run countless missions together. They had never been apart for more than a few days. After today, Wes realized he might never see his friend again.

Shakes looked as if he wanted to say more, thought better of it, then changed his mind again. "Wes . . ."

"Yeah?"

"About Nat."

"Yeah?"

Shakes made a long to-do about putting away his gear and hiking up his bag. "Nothing . . . just take care. Don't spoil my wedding, you hear? Liannan will be pissed if she doesn't have a bridesmaid. And who's going to be my best man?"

"You're planning a wedding?" Wes almost laughed, then saw that Shakes was serious.

"I was thinking three hundred people. At the Apple. You know, their fancy new ballroom, back in New Vegas." Shakes chuckled. "Just kidding. But we're doing it. She already said yes, you know. Wherever it is, whatever this world looks like after Nat casts the spell, we'll tie the knot. So you guys better make it."

Wes marveled at his friend's sunny optimism. Only Vincent "Shakes" Valez would set out on an impossible journey with very little chance of success, with a wedding in mind. "You got it," said Wes. "I'll plan the bachelor party with Brendon."

Shakes laughed and slapped him on the back. "That's my man."

They walked together to the front of the house where the rest of the team was assembled. Liannan was already atop her white winged horse. Shakes climbed up behind her. Wes found Nat hugging Brendon.

"Good luck, Wes," said the smallman, offering his hand. Brendon had aged in a week, shriveled, as if he were only half of himself now that Roark was gone.

Wes clasped his hand. "Godspeed, Donny. We'll see you at Shakes's wedding."

"What wedding?" asked Nat, raising her eyebrows.

"Haven't you heard? After all this, Shakes is making a respectable woman out of our Liannan." He grinned as he helped Brendon upon his pony.

Liannan blushed while Shakes smiled proudly. A ring glittered on her finger, and she waved it in the light. Leave it to

Shakes to find a jeweler in this place. Then she was back to business, addressing the two of them. "Use the speaking stone to find us once you're out of the red world. Hopefully, we will have located Eliza by then and delayed her from reaching the Gray Tower."

She clucked at her horse, and the winged cavalry sped away into the clouds, through a new portal that the sylphs had created that would allow them to return to the gray world. The portal closed behind the last rider, leaving the sky as seamless as before.

"Here goes nothing, huh?" he said to Nat, who was holding the reins of a beautiful stallion. The horse would take them to the ruins of Apis and return to the village on its own.

He made a cradle with his hands and helped Nat on the horse, then hoisted himself up on the saddle as well. "Is this all right?" he asked, as he wrapped his arms around her waist.

She nodded and tugged at the reins, leading the horse out of the grounds and through the village, toward the road that would take them back to the fallen city.

"Do you plan on talking to me at all on this journey of ours?" he asked. "Because it'll be awful lonely if you don't."

She turned to face him abruptly, her cheeks crimson. "I'm sorry. I've been rude."

Actually she had been worse than rude, she'd been so polite it killed him. This was Nat, who had kissed him on the ferryboat, who had risked her life to save his own, and who had shared her drakonfire with him. It just didn't make sense. She knew how he felt about her and until now he'd believed she felt the same.

"Will you tell me what's wrong?" he asked, leaning in to whisper in her ear, and he swore he could feel her skin tingle.

Every sense of his own was on alert, with her back against his chest, his hands around her tiny waist. He could have held on to the saddle but he wanted any excuse to touch her. Her soft hair tickled his cheek.

"I can't," she said.

"You can't or you won't?" His heart beat painfully in his chest, and he wanted to scream, to shake some sense into her, bring her back to him somehow. What happened? How was it possible she had changed her mind about him? But why? And why now?

"Let's not argue," Nat said quietly. "It's a long ride."

And just as he'd predicted, it was a silent one.

They reached the still-smoking ruins of Apis by the late afternoon and said good-bye to their mount. Wes wished the journey had been longer, as now there was no reason to be so close to her.

The city loomed above them like the hulking trashbergs of the ruined Pacific. There was nothing but wreckage, smoke and broken stone, singed cloth, shattered glass.

Wes studied the map that Liannan had given them. "There should be some kind of gate around here," he said.

Nat was three paces ahead of him. "This is it," she said, approaching a shattered wall. "It used to float hundreds of feet in the air."

He folded back the map. He vaguely remembered the city

in the sky, but he'd assumed it had been built on a mountain-top that he just couldn't see. "It floated?"

"Yeah, the whole city, high above the clouds."

"Bad idea. Cities should stay on the ground." He was glad she was at least talking to him, and he wanted to make the conversation last.

Nat shrugged. "Maybe. It was beautiful, though. You had to walk across a void to enter. I was supposed to take a leap of faith, create a bridge with my mind." She shook her head ruefully. "I don't know . . . it didn't work."

"Well, the only leap you'll need to make is over a few broken rocks. If we can even find the door," Wes said with a smile. He examined the pile of rubble before them. "I see a few pieces of the wall, but no gate, no opening. It might be blocked."

The remains of Apis resembled a mountain of loosely piled stones. He could make out some of the remaining structures—a tower here, a rotunda there, a bridge smashed at midpoint, a ring of turrets, a golden dome, a crenelated parapet, statues with missing limbs—all of it half covered in rubble.

The earth shook beneath them and Nat stumbled. Wes caught her before she fell.

"Sorry," she said, pushing away quickly before he could enjoy it too much. "I'm not used to earthquakes."

"Not an earthquake. I think the city's settling. Half of it crumbled when it hit the earth, but the rest of it's still falling apart. Each floor's buckling, falling on the one beneath it and crushing the one below. We need to hurry or this conservatory might be gone by the time we reach it."

They picked their way through the pile, still looking for a way inside. Nat fell silent again and avoided his gaze.

Wes studied the destruction, followed a line of broken stones, and spied a massive stone arch, still preserved, and a dark corridor beyond it.

"There!" he said, but Nat was already hurrying into it.

They plunged into the darkness. The tunnel was silent as a tomb, for it was one, filled with burnt bodies and blackened skeleton bones, the remains of the citizens of Apis who had failed to escape before the fires.

"Wait up," he called, coming along beside her, but she brushed him off, turning abruptly down a dark corridor. He could barely see her through the dust and smoke.

He followed her into the tunnel and out into the light. They were inside the city at last and had emerged into what had once been a ring of trees, a pine forest, it looked like. Most were burnt and twisted, their needles turned to kindling. Nat was standing in the middle of the charred trees.

"The conservatory shouldn't be far from here," she said, over the crack of stones splitting. The air smelled of death and blood.

Wes consulted the map again and Nat looked over his shoulder. "We're here." She pointed to what looked like the forest. They had gone about the half the distance to the conservatory, walking mostly aboveground or near the surface. When they left the forest, they would need to plunge deeper into the city, into subterranean passages that might be blocked or destroyed.

She moved away from him.

"Is it something I said? Or do you not like my new sylph cologne?" he joked. "Scent of forest. Mossy."

"No," she said flatly, and turned away, obviously not in the mood for his jokes.

Wes watched her leave him. If only she would tell him what was wrong, because something had to be. It was all wrong, especially if Nat wasn't amused by him anymore. He'd enjoyed making her laugh and he missed it. Either she'd lost her sense of humor, or not only did she no longer find him funny, but she no longer cared for him at all.

The possibility was too awful even to contemplate. Until then, Wes had never realized there was another way to lose your love; not through violence, separation, or death, but indifference.

And if Nat didn't love him anymore, what was there to live for? Wes brooded on this question all the way to the conservatory.

17

ALL SHE COULD THINK TO DO WAS RUN
away from Wes, and so she did. It was too hard to be so close
to him without spilling everything—her fears, her anxiety, the
secret that Nineveh had told her. This way, he would live and
leave her before it was too late. Even if the thought was so
hurtful it made her ill, she knew she was doing the right thing.

I will not be the cause of your death, she thought, as she ran
deep into the stony depths of the city. *I will not destroy you with
my dark fate.*

She would protect him, as she had tried to protect Vallonis.
She would keep him safe from harm. Safe from her.

No matter that every time he looked at her, confusion and
pain in his brown eyes, she wanted to kiss it away. She would
be strong, for him.

She heard his footsteps behind her, but he did not call her
name. Already it was working, she thought, for as she withdrew he pulled away. Just like the fraying of the bond of her
drakon.

Nat tried to concentrate on finding her way to the conservatory. The path was littered with broken marble statues, except unlike the statues back in New Vegas, these had no bases, no plinths underneath. Like the city, the statues must have floated in the air. She imagined elegant arrangements of marble sculptures hanging like clouds in the galleries. It must have been gorgeous, but now they were all smashed. Every bit of marble was chipped. Some were missing hands or feet or both. A marble head idled in a corner, bodiless.

She hurried through a corridor of glass, trying not to slip on the smooth surface.

"Are you sure this is the way?" Wes called, the hard surface of the tunnel shattering his voice into a dozen echoes. The rounded surface of the glass bent the light, making strange reflections, distorting their reflections, twisting them into odd shapes.

"Yes," she said tersely, her voice ringing in the corridor. She had memorized the map. This was the way, she was sure of it. She led them down into the lower levels, into the dark corridors that led into the heart of the conservatory. She tried not to be distracted by the broken pieces of art all around her or by the boy who was hurrying to catch up to her.

"Slow down," said Wes. "I don't want to crash through the glass." His voice sounded as if he were very far away now, but she didn't turn.

"Nat, seriously, let up! Are you trying to lose me?"

Yes, but not in the way you think. But she stopped. "I'm here. Hurry!" She heard his footsteps coming closer and she raised her voice. "I don't know if you care, but this is our only chance at saving this snow globe. So excuse me if I don't slow down. We've got work to do," she said crossly.

She kept going. When she finally turned around to check where he was, he was right behind her and their bodies collided in the darkness. She reached out for him instinctively, and when she fell he was there to catch her.

When he looked down at her, his face was an angry red. "I care. All I do is care. You're the one who—"

"Who what?"

"Never mind."

"Who cares more for this world than your feelings? Is that what you wanted to say to me? Because you're right," she snapped.

His face was burning, a bright scarlet.

Kill every ounce of his love, she told herself. *Do it. Let him turn away, let him forget you; it will save his life if he leaves you. Push him away.*

"That's not what I wanted to say," he said hoarsely. "I know what you have to do, and I'm here to help you do it. You can't get rid of me that easily, although it seems as if you want nothing more, and I don't understand why."

He locked his eyes on hers. He wasn't angry, she realized. Just sad, and he was still holding her although she'd already found her footing. Neither of them had noticed as it felt so natural.

They stared at each other for what felt like an infinite moment in time, and when he pulled her closer to him, she did not push him away. He was right, he smelled like their sylph hosts, like moss and sunshine, but underneath, he was still Wes, with his boyish, earthy smell that she loved.

"Come on, Nat, what is it?" he whispered. "You can tell me." His hands rubbed her back, tangled in her hair.

He bent down, and his face was so close to hers that all she had to do was lift her lips to his and everything would be like it had been.

I want you more than anything. I can't do this alone, she wanted to tell him. She would explain and he would assure her that everything would be all right.

Except he was wrong. Nothing was all right.

And yet she wanted to kiss him more than anything in the world, maybe more than she wanted to *fix* the world, and maybe that was why they were all doomed.

She fluttered her eyelids, unwilling to pull away but knowing she had to. She felt his lashes on her cheek, felt his lips part open.

But instead of kissing him she opened her eyes, alarmed at a sudden insight. Why was his face red if he wasn't angry?

Wes opened his eyes, too, disappointed. "What?"

"The corridor . . . it's lit up . . . I didn't notice . . . everything is red." She pushed his hands away, thankful she had found the strength to do so.

He looked around, alert, a soldier once more. "Yeah."

"There's a light somewhere. It's coming from there," she said. "Come on."

Together they ran through the corridors of glass, until they found the source of the light.

The chamber was huge, bigger than any room she'd ever seen. It was as wide as one of the casino floors back in New Vegas, as tall as a skyscraper, taller even perhaps. They entered at the tower's midpoint. One of the glass-walled corridors led them to a suspended walkway, and that walkway led to a suspended platform in the center of the conservatory.

High above, a glass ceiling revealed blue skies. Though shattered in spots, the glass was mostly intact. It was rosy in color, but there were shades of yellow and magenta mixed into the crystal. It was magical.

Nat felt awkward and out of place, and maybe she was. She had not earned the right to enter Apis; she failed the test. *I'm just a thief, a burglar come to pilfer the last of the city's magic.*

In the far corner of the room was a door whose handle was a golden drakon claw identical to the one she wore as a charm around her neck. Faix's mark.

"I'm going to open it," she said, her hand on the claw handle. "Last chance. Maybe you should get out of here. I can take care of it myself."

But Wes would have none of it. "I told you, I'm not going anywhere. Stop wasting time," he said, looking up at the dome. The sound of cracking glass rattled the chamber.

The glass shook, and if it fell they would be hit by a thousand tiny needles. There was enough glass in the ceiling to bury the two of them if it broke while they stood underneath it.

She put a hand on the handle, and as she did, the claw clamped it in its grip, digging its sharp edges into the palm of her hand, startling her. She tried to release her hold, but the claw held her fast, hard enough to draw blood.

She kept her hold on the handle and turned. "Here goes nothing," she said, as the door opened.

There was a flash of red as the world exploded into flames. She didn't even have time to call for Wes before she slipped through the doorway.

She was no longer holding the door handle, no longer standing at the doorway; she was flying through the heat and flame, the fire surging all around, lost in the storm of the inferno.

When she opened her eyes, she was no longer in the vast glass-enclosed conservatory of Apis.

The air smelled different; it tasted different. She was in a dark forest, and the silence was complete and eerie. There were no creatures rustling in the trees, no wind rustling leaves, nothing but the echo of her footsteps. When she looked up, there were stars in the sky, but they were not the stars she knew in the skies of Vallonis. These didn't follow the same patterns. They were not her stars. This was an alien place, another world. Another universe. Another place and time. The ruins of Atlantis and Avalon.

And she was alone. "Wes?" she called, frightened. Where was he? Had she lost him? Was he back in the conservatory? Or trapped in the red haze? Her heart thumped in fear. "Wes! Wes, where are you?"

In reply, a thunderous roar shook the forest floor.

Nat froze. She knew that sound.

It was the battle cry of a drakon and it was headed her way.

18

BEFORE HE COULD FIND NAT, WES watched a pillar of flame descend from the sky, arcing like a bolt of fury, filling the air with smoke, blinding him with light. The flames cut a path through the trees, racing toward him as they consumed everything in their path. The heat was so intense his face felt as if it were already burning. Red and orange sparks danced around him, and wisps of flame lapped at his shirt and pants, threatening to stick. It was too late to run, the only option was to fight, and so Wes pushed back against the drakonfire with his own power, managing to deflect enough of it to avoid being burned by the initial strike.

Wes dove for the cover of tall trees, hoping to lose the drakon. There was nothing else he could do. He couldn't fight the creature with a blade or a gun, and his magic was tapped out for now.

Above him, the creature's wings made a terrible sound. Torrents of hot air whistled through the trees. Flame spiraled in all directions. He heard an intake of air followed by the sound of a great exhalation as the drakon lit the forest with its flame once more. The fire spread from tree to tree, igniting leaves and branches, sending sparks flying and trees crashing to the ground. The successive bursts lit up the night and the forest floor came alive with flame. A great yellow wave of fire rolled up to a great height and crashed around him.

Nowhere was safe. He had to run.

Wes stumbled over fallen branches and logs. He leapt over jagged rocks, wondering whether Nat was here somewhere, lost amid the flames. He looked for her, but the forest was aflame and she was nowhere to be seen. He cursed himself for letting her fall through the doorway alone.

He ran deeper and deeper into the dark woods, hoping for a reprieve, a moment to catch sight of Nat, but the drakon would not rest. It was crisscrossing the forest, setting everything on fire. The flames drew nearer, and there seemed to be no escape. Wes readied himself for the final blow. The fire approached. He tried to push back against it again, to control it as he had done a moment ago, but nothing happened. In a moment, the drakon would light him up like tinder. He'd be nothing but toast. Burnt toast.

He waited for the death stroke, for the drakon to breathe fire down on him. A moment passed. Nothing. He heard only the beating of his heart, and in the distance the sound of the drakon's wings.

It was fading. *Did the drakon spare me?* No. Wes knew better. The creature could have killed him easily, but someone had prevented its strike.

Someone had caught its attention.

"Nat!" he cried.

In the distance, he saw a figure darting between the trees, and went after it. "Nat!" he called again, certain that the drakon was nearly upon her. "Wait!"

He readied his weapon as he ran through the dark forest, following the blaze, the sparkle of lights from the distance that could only be fire from drakonflame. The trees were twisted and ancient, long dead, the bark fossilized into stone. There was no wind, but he felt a chill. The forest was dark, the flames were behind him, and everything was rendered in shades of black and gray, like a charcoal drawing.

There was nothing living in this world, and Wes knew this was the future of their own if Nat was unable to recast the spell.

Another fiery blast came from the north side of the dead forest. She was alone out there. He should have stood his ground and not let his pride get in the way when they were quarreling earlier. He was paying for it now.

"Nat!" he called. "Where are you? Can you hear me?"

Fire lit the sky, washing out the stars and blinding him briefly.

The drakon was close, and he hoped that meant Nat would be as well.

A scream broke the smoky silence—*Nat?* He ran faster, stumbling over roots and rocks.

The forest was darker now, and he couldn't see in front of himself. He was lost, alone in a strange, dead world. There were no flickering lights on the horizon.

Where were they?

He saw neither Nat nor the drakon, but when a shadow

moved, he saw something else: a hooded figure, not ten steps ahead of him, holding a gleaming blade.

Wes took a step back, careful not to make any noise, his military training allowing him to retreat as silently as if he had never been there.

There was someone else in the forest with them. Someone dangerous. He had to find Nat.

19

THE DRAKON BORE DOWN UPON NAT, and she ran deeper into the forest, knocking into dead trees, pushing through the dense undergrowth. Thorns snagged at her clothes, and dry branches cracked beneath her feet. She did not fear its fire, but she had no defense against its mighty jaws. She knew its talons could tear her to pieces while its teeth could grind her into dust. So Nat ran from the drakon, using the forest as cover, twisting through the trees and the undergrowth. The creature roared in frustration. Smoke filled the air, and the haze obscured her vision. The fire could not harm her—she was made of flame—but it did confuse her senses. In the swirling cloud of ash and smoke, she lost track of where she was and where she was headed.

I'm lost, she thought. Everywhere she looked there were more trees, all of them dark. The sky was hazy, and the only sound she heard was the flapping of the drakon's wings. The *flap-flap* of its wings intensified; the creature was near. Nat steeled herself for the fight.

Where are you? She studied the sky. She wanted a chance to speak to it before it killed her. But what could she do? How could she prove that she was worthy of its time?

She had been running away, she realized, acting as a victim, and there was nothing drakons despised more than weakness.

"Here!" she called, stepping out of the trees and raising her hands to the sky. Smoke from the fires swirled around her waist, stretching up to her waving arms, but she was certain the creature would see her. She knew it would acknowledge her challenge.

She was a rydder.

Nat called again, "Here! Face me!"

At first she heard only the echo of her words and the crackle of the flames. Then the *clap* of the drakon's wings came again, louder. Without warning, the creature was upon her. It fell from the sky at a frightful pace, descending upon a powerful torrent of air. The rush of wind extinguished the fire and sent sand and rocks tumbling into her face. Even the black clouds of smoke dispersed when the drakon landed.

Settling to the earth, the creature folded its wings and raised its sinuous neck. Through nictitating membranes, its red eyes shot her a frightful glare. She met its fierce gaze with a fiery stare of her own. A moment earlier the thing had been ready to tear her limb from limb. Now it just regarded her with something like curiosity.

The red drakon dwarfed Drakon Mainas, its scales a bloody scarlet, its eyes garnets gleaming in the night. Its scales were mottled with streaks of black. They were torn in spots and littered with scabs and cuts, wounds that had only half healed. Even its claws were chipped in spots and cracked. The creature looked as old as the world itself, older perhaps. Ancient.

"WHO COMES TO DISTURB MY REST?" the drakon rumbled, catching her off guard. "WHO COMES TO THE RED LANDS?"

"I am Anastasia Dekesthalias, the Resurrection of the Flame. The one who has returned, the one who will light the world anew," she said, keeping her voice even.

"So you say. A drakonrydder, are you? I feel the fire within your soul. And yet . . ." The drakon reared up and let its long spiky tail snake around its side, contemplating her words. "Know this. Drakontongue is the language of the ether. Its breath forges worlds, its blood makes mountains. You cannot lie to a drakon and a drakon never lies."

"I haven't lied to you," said Nat.

"And yet the stench of lies surrounds you," he said. "Why have you come to the Red Lands?"

"For assistance," said Nat, kneeling in front of the magnificent creature.

The great red drakon snorted and released two clouds of smoke. "And where is it that you have come from?"

"I have come from beyond the Blue, across the black oceans and ruined lands."

The drakon slithered around the forest, letting its tail wrap around a tree. "What kind of assistance? And why do you think I shall offer it? Who sent you?"

"Faix Lazaved, Messenger to the Queen of Vallonis."

"Faix the Liar?" the drakon roared.

Nat took a step back, frightened by the creature's sudden rage.

"It is too late to punish the drau, but perhaps I can take my revenge on you," the drakon said in a menacing and smoky whisper.

"You will not harm me," she said, her voice commanding even as she trembled before the beast. "Faix did you no ill; he meant you no harm. He only meant to save you from the corruption that had befouled our world."

The drakon leaned down, its fangs inches from Nat's face; she could feel the heat from the furnace inside him. One blast and she would be burned to ashes and dust. "Drakonrydder, are you? Then where is your drakon? You are a liar just as he was a liar!"

"Faix was no liar," she said staunchly. "And if you stop roaring and listen to me, I can explain."

The drakon swatted its tail and felled the tree. It released a stream of flame and turned to Nat, its red eyes blazing. "FAIX LAZAVED IS A LIAR, HIS QUEEN IS A LIAR, AND YOU ARE NOT WHAT YOU SAY! LEAVE ME BE! RETURN WHENCE YOU CAME!"

"I will not!" she cried. "Burn me if you don't believe I tell the truth!" She closed her eyes and braced for the onslaught. She felt the wind whistle across her arm and knew the drakon had drawn in a great breath. It meant to breathe flame, to surround her in a cloud of smoke and ash. Its talons tensed, its muscles stretched tight as it readied itself to pounce. The creature shivered, but it did not attack. Instead the drakon only screeched and wailed, unable to hurt her, for she was not lying.

Nat shielded her eyes from the heat of the drakon's gaze, feeling it boring into her soul and finding her wanting. She opened one eye. "Are you done?"

The drakon huffed, clearly annoyed but unwilling to give in, almost like a crotchety old man. "You say you are the Resurrection of the Flame, the one who was promised. And yet your soul is a web of confusion and doubt. You will not be able to cast the Archimedes spell with a splintered heart and a weak will," it rumbled. "You will fail as Faix failed."

It was right about her, and the thought left her cold, but still she attempted to argue with the beast. "But his failure was not of his doing. He did not know why the spell did not work."

The drakon slithered to rest next to her, folding its legs under its belly. Its voice had lost its anger. "Perhaps. But I do."

"You know why the spell did not hold?"

"Aye."

Nat waited for it to explain, sensing that the drakon wanted nothing more than to tell her its story.

Sure enough, it did.

"One hundred and eleven years ago, Faix Lazaved sought the *Archimedes Palimpsest*, to return magic to its rightful place in the world. To create the third age of Avalon: the city of Apis.

"Every citizen of Vallonis dedicated their life to the task of finding the world-making scroll. When it was found, he brought it to the Queen. Nineveh cast the spell, calling on all the elements of creation and the wilds beyond. For a moment it appeared she had triumphed. But instead, the ice came, and with it, the corruption that turned magic against itself." The drakon blew smoke across the treetops. "As you are aware, the spell requires a great sacrifice from its caster."

Nat nodded. Faix had told her about the Queen's sacrifice, about how she had given the life of their son to create Apis.

"NO," the drakon said, reading her thoughts. "She made no such sacrifice."

"That cannot be. I was told—"

"Lies. They lied to you, Natasha. They lied to their people. They lied to me. They said they had given their son to the spell, but they lied. The sacrifice was not made. The spell did not hold.

"The world fell into darkness, as the spell that should have saved the world destroyed it. It brought the ice and gave birth to this ruined world, to this starless sky, to the corruption and sickness that destroys the magic folk of Vallonis, and those you call marked. Faix and his Queen are the reason your world is gray."

She stared at the drakon.

The drakon glared back. "Faix and his Queen are the reason I am trapped in this place."

"But the sylphs believe Faix put you here, to keep you safe."

"Another lie. He caged me here because I knew the truth. Kept me here so that I would not tell others what I knew." The drakon shrugged, its scales rolling dramatically across its shoulders.

She thought of Faix and his quiet determination, his

solitude and his sadness. How well did she know her friend? What secrets had he been hiding?

"Although perhaps he did retain hope. He found the last remaining drakonrydder, after all. Perhaps he hoped that somehow the last drakonrydder would undo the evil she had unleashed upon the world. Are you aware of what is required of you?" the drakon asked. "Are you ready for the test?"

"Yes," she said stoutly. "I am ready." This was not a lie. She was ready to give her life to the spell, ready to sacrifice herself, to light the world anew.

She would give everything. She would die, so all could live.

"Ah, but that is not the sacrifice," the drakon said smugly, rumbling toward her, its red eyes flashing once more.

Nat stopped.

Oh.

Of course.

She had it all wrong.

She believed that the spell only required the sacrifice of her life, but now she saw the truth. The Queen had been asked to sacrifice her son.

To save the world, she would have to sacrifice those she loved.

You will kill them all.

You will bring death to everyone around you, death to all whom you love.

If you stay with him, you will destroy him.

Wes.

He will die because of me. Because he loves me.

Her lip trembled. Her eyes glazed with tears. This was not what she had signed up for, this was too much, she couldn't do it, she wouldn't. She was just an orphan from the gray lands. She was no one. She was nobody.

The drakon stared back, into her heart, into the darkness inside. "You are not ready to make this sacrifice."

"I cannot."

"Then the world is doomed," he pronounced.

"There is no other way?"

The drakon did not reply. "The rules of making were bound in the dawn of the world. There is no changing them."

Subject unable to love, she remembered the words from her file at MacArthur Med. Subconsciously, she'd known she was supposed to be alone in the world, so that when she reached her destiny, her greatest sacrifice would be her own life. Somehow she had known what she would have to do and had closed herself off from all feeling, because deep down, she knew her life would lead to that Gray Tower. She should never have allowed herself to know him, to love Ryan Wesson; she had only sealed his doom with her own.

"But do not despair, Anastasia Dekesthalias," the red drakon said, unexpectedly sympathetic.

"Why? Is there is hope yet?" she asked.

The drakon echoed the words Liannan spoke to her earlier. "There is always hope."

She stared at the drakon. "You said you were there when Nineveh cast the spell. You are no ordinary drakon, are you?"

"Observant."

"Were you ever Faix's drakon?"

The drakon snorted. "If you are asking if I took him as a rydder, yes, briefly. He was young, promising, and Vallonis needed a warrior."

"Will you help me on my quest?" she asked, bowing low.

The drakon sighed. "You will find no war with me, drakonrydder."

"But you shall find war with me," said a voice in the darkness. "For you are misguided as usual. There is no more hope for Avalon. Nor its champion."

Nineveh stepped from the shadows, brandishing a sword and removing her hood to show them her face.

20

HIDDEN IN THE DARKNESS, A FEW STEPS
away from where Nat and the drakon were conversing, Wes
saw two things happen at once: The Queen emerged from
the forest, golden armor covering her from helmet to shimmering sandals, a halo of white illuminating her brow. She
wore a gleaming shield on one arm, and bore a great sword
with the other. At the same time the Queen appeared, Nat
swiftly turned to the red drakon, the creature bowed, and she
leapt upon it, landing in the crook of its shoulders. Before
the Queen could raise her weapon, the drakon and its rydder
were airborne.

Its wings made whirlwinds of ash and dust rise into the
air. The Queen shaded her eyes. Wes saw an opportunity and
took it. He rushed into the clearing, weapon raised, ready to
defend Nat. His mind was swimming from everything he'd
overheard, and he wasn't sure what to think of Nat or the
drakon or what they had said to each other. What sacrifice?
What was the drakon talking about? What did Nat have to do
for the spell?

There was no time to mull things over, as the Queen met his attack with one of her own.

"You've served your purpose," Nineveh sneered. "Do not try to fight me. It will only hasten your death."

She drew back her blade, leaving herself open to his attack. With a cry, Wes hacked at her with his trusty axe, his blade glancing off her golden armor. He drew back his weapon in time to catch her sword. The blade bit into the axe handle, taking a chunk out of the wood. She motioned to withdraw the blade, but the sword had caught on the handle of his axe. She cursed, but for a moment her sword was lodged in the handle. Neither could strike with their weapon, so he put both hands on the axe and used it as a ram. He threw her backward and she stumbled, freeing their weapons. Drawing back his axe, he struck before she could parry. The axe bit into her armor, rending a narrow gash, but the Queen was unharmed. There must be some enchantment that made the armor impenetrable, he thought. No matter. He struck at the exposed flesh of her hand. The blade made contact and the Queen shrieked, losing her sword as she ducked a second attack. Before she could recover, he swung again, bringing his axe up against her throat. She might be a Queen, but she was no warrior. Wes held the blade to her skin.

She laughed, and when it touched her, the axe turned into fire in his hands. He threw it off as quickly as could, but the fire left burn marks on his hands. The blade tumbled through the air, but before it hit the earth, it turned into steam, evaporating into a cloud of white.

"I made that blade, as I made everything in Vallonis," said

the Queen, her teeth gritted. "Did you think you could use it against me?"

"Will you have a child fight your battle?" she yelled to the drakon. "Coward!" Nineveh taunted the creature, her voice cutting through the silence like fang through flesh.

In answer, the red drakon returned, Nat upon its back, gouts of white-hot flame pouring down upon the land. The heat was so intense Wes had to shield his face; he gathered what magic he had to push back against the drakonfire. He took a step back, but the Queen stood her ground. She locked eyes with Nat and met the flames with a haughty gaze. Like water bouncing off a stone, the fire splashed upon her shield. Her armor made the flames curve around the metal, without ever touching it. As Wes already knew, the suit was enchanted, designed to deflect drakonfire as well as axes.

The drakon roared its frustration and soared into the sky, its body making a hazy, red silhouette against the stars, blocking out their light before descending once more, gliding toward the forest and the Queen who waited, sword raised. Wes saw Nat hunched low on the drakon's back, her eyes flashing, her hair whipping in the breeze.

This time, the drakon did not breathe flame. It hovered, beating its wings. The flapping made trees tumble and boulders spin. Nat sat upright upon the drakon's back. She faced the Queen without fear or hesitation. Though Wes could not hear the words, he saw her whispering to the drakon, readying their attack. The drakon came closer, its wings flapping in increasingly powerful motions. The air swirled around the Queen. A strong wind became a hurricane of immeasurable strength. The roar alone was deafening. Wes stumbled backward to avoid the winds, but there was nowhere for the Queen to go. The drakon had focused the full force of its mighty wings upon her. A final, powerful gust knocked the Queen to her knees, her armor crunching as it struck the earth.

She was distracted, perhaps injured. Wes cast about for anything he could use in the fight. He had no other weapon, nothing but his hands.

Maybe I can distract her, wrestle her to the ground.

The winds abated and Wes lunged for the Queen, but she was already gone, and had recovered her weapon.

Nineveh threw herself upward, hurtling toward Nat and the drakon. In a blur of motion, she thrust her blade into its glistening red scales. There was nothing he could do, no way to stop her.

It was all over in an instant.

The drakon roared in pain, its cries echoing across the dark night.

Again the Queen plunged her sword into the drakon's hide, and the creature faltered, sending Nat flying to the ground.

21

NAT STRUCK THE EARTH WITH A MIGHTY thump, and something snapped as she hit the forest floor. She felt a broken branch beneath her, but it could have easily been her spine that had shattered. She hurt all over and her head was spinning. It wasn't the first drakon she had fallen from and she guessed it wouldn't be the last, but it still hurt. Her ears rang. Above the din, there was a second noise, the sound of metal crunching against dry leaves, footsteps coming closer.

Where's my sword?

Cold steel touched her neck. She looked down and recognized the steely black edge of her blade. Someone else had found her blade.

Nineveh loomed over her, holding Liannan's father's sword. *The Red Lands are haunted by the dead,* Liannan had warned. Why was the Queen here? Did she know they would come this way? She must have.

Nat was on her knees. She didn't know if she could stand. The fall had rattled her senses, made all her muscles go stiff.

If she tried to get up and face the Queen, she might fall on her face; so Nat wrapped her fingers around the drakonbone blade and tried to push the sword away, no matter that the edge cut into her skin.

The Queen scoffed. "You don't have the strength," she said. "Relent."

Nat shook her head, but when blood dribbled down her hand, she did relent. She was in no shape to fight. *I need help. Where's Wes? Is he all right?* Had the Queen hurt him? Nat gritted her teeth angrily.

"Why are you doing this?" Nat choked. "What purpose does it serve?"

Nineveh bared her glistening white teeth. Both hands were on the sword now and she kept it close to Nat's neck. When she spoke, her voice oozed with mockery. "Once upon a time I believed as you do, that I could fix this world, that I could bring magic back into the gray lands and usher in the third golden age of Vallonis, an eternal kingdom. I was wrong."

"Because you never made the sacrifice the spell required," Nat said, though it hurt when she spoke. The sword was still at her throat. "Even if Faix believed you did. He believed you sacrificed your son." Faix didn't know, Nat was sure. He believed their child was dead and had mourned him. The drakon had been wrong about Faix. The Queen was the only liar.

Nineveh confirmed it. "Faix believed what I wanted him to believe. If he knew the truth, he would have sacrificed our son! *Our son!*"

A realization dawned on Nat. "Your son is alive, isn't he?"

The Queen didn't answer. She pressed her lips together

and drew back her sword as if she was about to strike. Nat coughed and pressed her hand to her throat. It came away wet with blood, stinging wildly. The pain clouded her thoughts, but Nat pushed it away. There was something important here, the secret at the heart of everything.

"If you didn't sacrifice him, then where is he?" Nat asked. "I think I know. You hid him away in our world. You sent him into the ice."

"For his survival," said the Queen. She put the sword to Nat's chin, but she did not strike her. "So that he could one day meet his destiny."

"And what is that?"

"The tower. He will succeed where I failed," rasped the Queen. "He is there now."

"Your son is Avo Hubik," said Nat suddenly. Avo did not dye his hair. He only pretended to, to mask his true nature, his true identity.

Avo did not pretend to be drau; he was drau.

He was marked, just like them. Did he know what he was? The scar above his eyebrow, just like Wes's scar. They were the same. The sword rested on Nat's chin, but the Queen didn't strike. Nat understood now that the Queen wasn't going to kill her. If she'd wanted her dead, she would have struck while Nat was on her knees, reeling from the fall.

"My son will finish what I started," the Queen continued. "The tower is his. He will shape the world in our image."

"Your son is a madman."

Nat's mind raced. The Queen sought Vallonis's annihilation; she wanted the destruction of that world to facilitate the birth of the next one. The world her son would command.

Eliza would destroy the tower while Avo would use its power for his own.

Not if I can help it, Nat vowed, even as the black sword was cold under her chin. There was no sign of the red drakon or of Wes.

Nineveh cried out to the dark. "Come out! Let us end this. If you submit, I will spare the drakonrydder!" It was the red drakon she wanted. That's why she hadn't killed Nat.

The great beast must have been close. The sound of wings beat nearby. It roared a long and terrible cry as it soared above the trees, coming around in a half circle before burying its claws in the dirt. The creature made a terrible thump when it landed, crying out as blood dripped from its chest, Nineveh's sword still lodged in its side. It walked with an awkward limp. "I am here, Nineveh." There was pain in the creature's voice, and Nat sensed that it was not just the pain of the creature's wound. She heard the pain of betrayal and years of suffering. She saw in the creature's eyes a sense of resignation, as if it were finally done fighting, done living, too. It lowered its head to the ground. "I yield."

Nineveh smirked. She raised her sword, and this time she did not hesitate. She brought the blade down upon the drakon in one swift and remorseless stroke. As the black blade streaked through the darkness, Nat caught a flicker of movement from the shadows, and her heart skipped a beat. She held her breath, hope thrumming wildly in her blood.

Nineveh swung the blade, Nat sucked air through her teeth, and the drakon gave one last fearsome roar.

The blade came down on the drakon, but it did not strike the creature's scales. A hair's width from the creature's neck, something struck the sword and it spiraled out of Nineveh's grip. She heard the crack of rifle fire. A cloud of smoke crept into her peripheral vision. It all happened in slow motion. The Queen's strike, the blade hurtling sideways out of her hands. Then there was a rustle in the trees. Nat turned to see Wes, standing to the side with a smoking rifle in his hand. The Queen saw him, too, and she saw the blade lying on the ground halfway between them.

The two eyed each other and both sprinted toward the sword.

Nat held her breath. Though her muscles ached from the fall, though each step forward sent shockwaves of pain arcing through her muscles, she paid them no attention. Nor did she care about the cut on her neck, the way it stung wildly when she'd started to run. There was only the sword. She fixed her eyes on the blade and threw herself toward it. One step, two. Then she leapt for it, stretching out her arms and gripping the handle before the Queen could wrap her long fingers around it.

She had it. Nat tumbled, rolling with the sword in her hand. She recovered, stood, and in one quick and decisive motion, before the Queen could flee, before she could cast a spell, Nat raised the general's weapon, the drakonbone sword of Alfarhome, and slashed the Queen's throat clean through.

22

NINEVEH FELL UPON THE GRAY STONES, limp as a sack of dirty laundry, blood flowing from her wound, gushing from her throat in a river of dark, spilling onto the deeper darkness of the ground underneath.

Wes heard the sword clatter as it fell from Nat's hand. They stared at each other in shock. He had heard everything that was said, had kept in the shadows, shocked at every word. Avo was drau? Of course. It all made sense now. He had known it, hadn't he? That he and Avo were alike somehow? He had sensed it, even when they were grunts. That Avo was more like him than Shakes ever was.

Wes had watched a show on the nets once, from the time before; it was an author, talking about his book, a book about criminals who had killed a family in cold blood. That was what it was called, *In Cold Blood*. The author explained in a quavering voice that he had been drawn to the story because the troubled murderer had come from the same background as he did. "And one day he stood up and went out the back door, while I went out the front."

Same background, different results.

One a celebrated author, the other a cold-blooded murderer.

Like him and Avo.

Hero and villain.

Two sides of the same coin.

"You all right?" he asked Nat, who was at the Queen's side. He picked up the sword and handed it back to her.

Nat put it back in its sheath and bent down to crouch next to the dying Queen but didn't answer him. Wes thought she was gone, that the life had poured out of her, but when Nat bowed, the Queen's eyes opened to narrow slits. She rolled over onto her back, revealing the wound on her throat. She was caked in blood and dirt. He wanted to look away, but he held himself still. The Queen was not done with them. She was not done with life. There was something she wanted.

"Emrys," Nineveh whispered. "Get Emrys." The Queen's ivory pallor was turning gray. Even her bright hair was dull, the light in her eyes fading to black.

Nat and Wes exchanged confused glances. "Who's Emrys?" she asked.

"I think she means the drakon," he said, his voice quiet. Both of them spoke in hushed tones.

"What do you want with him?" Nat asked. There was anger in her voice, but she tempered it with respect. Though Nineveh had betrayed them, though they could not trust her, she did pity her in her last moments.

The Queen grimaced, tried to sit up but failed. "Emrys," she said again. "Get me Emrys." Her voice was quieter now, her eyelids drooping, her every motion slow and languid. Soon, she'd be gone.

Wes nodded. One last wish for a dying woman. He could do that. He saw no harm in it. "I'll go."

He didn't know why he was doing it, but maybe it was because he was tired of death, tired of fighting. And he was curious, too, why Nineveh sought the company of one who vanquished her.

"Be careful," Nat called.

He looked over his shoulder.

She had a hand on the pommel of her sword, her cheeks were streaked with grime, and her dark hair was tangled and matted. But nothing could diminish her beauty in his eyes.

She still cared for him, too. The façade, whatever walls she had put up around her heart, they were crumbling.

"You, too," he said. "Keep an eye on her."

When he'd fired his rifle at the sword, the red drakon had been right there, right beside them. But it must have fled at the sound of gunfire. He'd been focused on Nat and the Queen and hadn't seen where the drakon had gone. He guessed it wasn't far away. The creature was wounded. He caught sight of bloodstains on the forest floor. There were large pools of red nestled among the leaves. There was too much blood for it to have come from a person. The great drakon was here.

He followed its bloody trail, moving quickly but cautiously. If he delayed, the Queen might be gone by the time he returned. If he moved too quickly, he might startle the creature. An injured drakon might not hesitate to attack if it saw him; it might light him up like a match and be done with it.

Wes moved slowly, crunching blackened branches and undergrowth beneath his feet, letting the drakon know that he approached. He found the red drakon, not far from Nat and the Queen. Like Nineveh, the creature seemed finished, but it was still holding on to life. Its arms were limp and its wings fell awkwardly at its sides. He doubted it could fly.

"She wants you," Wes said. "Nineveh's dying. It's her last wish."

The drakon opened one of its eyes.

"So, you are the one." The creature wheezed when it spoke. Wes could barely understand it.

"The one?"

"The child of Vallonis." The creature opened its maw, sputtering, spitting wisps of flame.

"It's not a title I was born with."

"I will ask you the same question I asked of the drakonrydder. Why are you here?" It coughed blood as it spoke.

"For her."

"Ah."

"What am I supposed to do?"

"Isn't it clear, Ryan Wesson? You're supposed to save the world and get the girl." The drakon's terrible laughter rumbled through the forest.

Wes raised an eyebrow. Sarcastic beast. Perhaps it was not yet finished.

"Actually. I was dispatched on an errand. She asked for you. Nineveh."

The drakon roared with sudden hatred. It rose up on its forelegs. Then it settled, blinking its eyes. Like Wes, the drakon seemed tired of fighting, tired of death. It gave what sounded like a long sigh. "I will speak to the Queen."

There was a rustle from the forest as the dying creature limped toward the fallen Queen. Its every step elicited a groan. It spit fire and roared when it saw her. A moment ago she'd held a sword above the creature's neck. She'd tried to kill the mighty drakon, but it was she who had felt the black sword's sting. Their positions were now reversed. The drakon towered over her, its wounds dripping blood, its eyes blazing when they alighted upon her fallen body. "Nineveh," it roared. The drakon spoke her name as if it were a curse.

"Emrys, please," Nineveh said, her voice weak. She was sitting up now, a piece of cloth pressed to her wound. She'd tried to stanch the wound, but had clearly failed. Her hands were red with blood, her skin pale. "Emrys, the drakonfire. I need it."

Wes understood now. The Queen was dying and she was asking for the life force, the same white flame that Nat had used to bring Wes back to life.

Wes reached for Nat's hand, and she accepted it.

He remembered the white fire that had sparked between their souls, the way it had warmed him, had brought him back from the cold abyss.

He shuddered.

Death was just another journey, but it was not one he wanted to take yet. And neither did the Queen.

"Please," said Nineveh, her voice growing shaky. "I can free you from this place. Save me and we can recast the spell together with Avo. Save me," she pleaded. She was desperate, her hands twitching, face white as bone. Wes was about to protest that she deserved no such mercy, but held his tongue. The drakon stared at the Queen, smoke pouring from its nostrils in long gray clouds. It opened its mouth, swallowed twice, but it gave her none of its flame. It gave her no assistance.

The Queen breathed out a long breath. "Won't you pity me?" she asked.

"No," it said softly. "You who have no pity in your heart will find no pity in others. You are done. Your fire has gone out."

Nineveh motioned to stand. She put her palms to ground and struggled to push herself up, but she only collapsed. The cloth fell from her neck, and blood dribbled down her chest. She looked up at them, but her eyelids were leaden and they sank slowly across her eyes, dimming her vision. When her eyes shut, Wes knew they would never open again. She fell to the earth. Her skin was gray, her body motionless. She died at the foot of the great drakon. She died a beggar, alone in the dirt, lying at the foot of one she had betrayed.

Wes let go of Nat's hand to kneel down by the Queen's side. He picked up her wrist to find a pulse. There was none. The skin was cold to the touch. The smell of death was all around her. He shook his head. "She's gone."

And so was the creature. The drakon lay motionless at her side. It heaved one last breath, a final sigh, then nothing. No rise and fall of breath. No fire and smoke. The blood at its chest was black. The creature lay there, unmoving. Nat hurried to its side; Wes stood and placed a hand on its head. When he touched it, he recoiled. It was moving, ever so slightly. The great red drakon was shrinking, shriveling. Soon its body was engulfed in a cloud of red sparks and white mist.

Nat stood; Wes stumbled backward.

Suddenly the drakon was no more.

In its place was an old man.

23

"WHO ARE YOU? WHAT ARE YOU?"
Nat asked, awed at the transformation.

The old man wore a red robe that was the same color as
the drakon and dotted with little scaly spots. His eyes were
tired, but she saw within them a distant glimmer, a light that
was slowly fading. This was clearly a man of importance, of
magic. An aura of great strength shimmered about him. He
must have been a powerful wizard in his time, greater than
any. But he was old now, his skin withered, his hands dotted
with liver spots, and his gray hair looked as if it hadn't been
cut in decades, centuries perhaps. He heaved a sigh. "Emrys
Myrddyn, Eternal Merlin of Avalon. Pleased to make your
acquaintance," he said, his voice sounding gruff. "Natasha?
This isn't a surprise, is it?" He coughed when he spoke.

She nodded. She'd guessed as much that there was something different about him, that he was no ordinary drakon.
Abruptly, she noticed the old man's eyes were red like the
drakon's.

"Hello, Ryan Wesson," he said, turning to Wes. His body trembled when he moved, and Nat feared he might collapse.

"My friends call me Wes," said Wes, shaking Emrys's hand. Wes's strong grip engulfed the old man's hand, making the wizard's fist look like a child's.

"Wes then," the wizard Emrys said. He turned without further addressing either of them, acting oddly, in the way Nat had seen people of advanced age sometimes act. She got the sense he was somewhere else, his thoughts distant. He knelt next to the Queen's dead body. He was still trembling a little, but this time it was grief and not age that stirred him. "Oh, Nineveh. How did it come to this?" He gently stroked the white fabric of her dress, brushing away a bit of the dirt, moving a fold of fabric to hide some of the blood.

"You loved her," Wes said and Nat knew he knew because the pain in his voice was familiar.

Emrys bent his head and nodded once as he closed the Queen's eyes. Nineveh was gone, dead, and Nat felt a pang of regret. The wizard cared for her, his emotions were clear. "She was my sister," he said. "And she has never agreed with me. Not in any iteration of Avalon in the infinite universe," he said sadly. "When I wanted to build libraries, she wanted walls. When I wanted to train scholars, she wanted to raise soldiers. On and on it went. I thought we should tear down the walls between the worlds, but she only wanted to strengthen them." He bowed his head again. "We are destined to oppose each other for eternity, it seems."

Wes grunted. "I know the feeling."

The wizard ignored him and closed his eyes. He stood, backing away from the body and motioning for them to do the same.

What is he doing? Nat wondered, while the wizard continued his whispering. He raised his hands and Nat felt a bit of heat. She recognized the fire of a drakon; she knew the way it felt on her skin. She put a hand on Wes's chest and motioned for him to retreat. The Queen's body was glowing now, shimmering with drakonflame. "Thus does Nineveh pass from this world. Let her spirit rest."

The great fire grew brighter and brighter, lighting the red world around them, like a sun rising in the darkness. The flame expanded, burning for a time before slowly sputtering out. Her embers drifted upward and into the stars. It was done. The body had vanished and not even an ash remained where it had once rested.

The Queen gone, Wes went to stand next to Nat. "I'm sorry I couldn't find you. I should never have let you walk through that doorway alone."

Nat shook her head. "It was my fault." She wished he would put his arm around her like he usually did. She missed having his hand in hers. She wanted the reassurance of his touch so badly she was almost shaking, but he didn't seem to notice.

The old man brushed his hands together. Despite his age, he still held great power—he had called the drakonflame as easily as Nat could have.

"Was she the one who cursed you into drakon form?" she

asked Emrys, trying to distract herself. It was all coming together now.

"Aye. And the curse includes not being able to tell anyone
about it. At least as a drakon I could move. One time she
turned me into a tree," he said wryly.

"I came for a drakon," she reminded him. "But now you are
no drakon and I fear I will never find mine."

She had failed, she thought. Eliza would burn down the
tower, or else Avo would seize its power for himself; either
way, they were all doomed.

Emrys studied his hands, as if surprised they were no longer claws. When he huffed, Nat almost expected smoke to
come out of his nostrils. He met Nat's stricken gaze with a
stern one of his own. "You do not need a drakon to retrieve
your own. You are its soul, its beating heart. Call your drakon,
and it will come to you."

"But the bond is broken," she argued. "It has accepted another rydder."

"Nonsense. A drakonbond is eternal. Listen and it will
hear your call. You have everything you need to get it back,"
Emrys told her. "You always have."

"Will you not help me with this task?" asked Nat.

"My time here is done," said Emrys. "I am needed
elsewhere."

"Where?"

"There are other worlds than these, my child, many different pasts, many diverging futures," he said. "The mirror of
Avalon holds infinites."

He stared at both of them sharply. "The future of this world is in your hands. Choose wisely."

"Is that it? Good-bye and good luck? We rescued you from a curse!" she called.

"And I am eternally grateful." Emrys turned to Wes. "Remember what I said, Wes. Remember how the story ends. Remember." He looked back at Nat. "Do not despair, drakon-rydder; perhaps we shall meet again. There are other worlds than these." With those parting words, he disappeared in a shower of red sparks.

"Wait! Emrys!" she called, but already the hidden universe was coming apart. The curse was broken, the drakon released from its cage.

Stars streaked across the sky; the earth rumbled underneath their feet. The dead trees shook into dust, the air became thin, and with a huge crash everything turned black.

24

THE DARKNESS GAVE WAY TO FAINT LIGHT, to the distant glow of embers and the sounds of breaking rock. Wes's eyes blinked open. His head was still spinning from the journey back from the Red, but he steadied himself and tried to get his bearings. They were back in the conservatory of Apis, except the red door was now charred and black like the rest of the city. The drakon's world was gone, collapsed like a dead star, burnt like the red door. He felt shaken, dizzy. He'd seen the death of the Queen and watched a great red drakon turn into an old man. He'd seen her ashes drift upward to the stars.

"Snap out of it," said Nat. He had forgotten she was beside him.

"What did he say to you? What do you have to remember?" she asked, her green eyes shining in the darkness. Her face and her voice helped steady him. She was the thing that kept him centered, and he knew he did the same for her.

"He said I should remember to save the world and get the girl." He whistled, coming alive as he saw her.

Nat laughed. "Is that so?"

"Yeah. And he's a wizard, so you know . . . a pretty wise man." Wes made a face. They'd both been through so much. It felt good to laugh.

"Wise guy more like it." But she was still smiling.

"Pretty big job if you ask me. Saving the world's probably easier, though," he said slyly. He moved closer, cleaning away the rest of the blood from her face with his own kerchief. As he wiped her face gently, it reminded him of the time he had bandaged her wounds on the trip out of New Vegas. Her ability to heal had been extraordinary. "You're not healing as quickly as before," he said, concerned.

"Maybe because Vallonis's power is diminishing," she said.

Wes kept his hand on her cheek, massaging the bruise.

He leaned in closer, forcing her to look him in the eye. "I heard what Emrys said to you—about the sacrifice? What sacrifice, Nat? What do you have to do? Tell me. I can help."

"You can't," she said dully. "It's my fate. Not yours."

"We'll share it," he told her, taking her hands in his, the way he had when she had brought him back to life on the ferry-boat, their fingers intertwining.

"NO!" she cried, looking horrified. "You can't!" She pulled her hand away.

It cut him to the quick.

"Look, Wes, nothing's wrong except the world is falling apart, and every minute we spend here puts everyone at risk."

"Liar," he said, remembering Emrys had called her one.

She bristled. "You can call me names but that's not helping anyone."

Wes decided to bluff. "If you don't want me around, that's fine. I'll leave you alone. We can go our separate ways," he said, even though he wasn't sure where that would be. Where would he go? The world was empty without her.

Nat exhaled in palpable relief. "Great."

"Fine," he said, his jaw clenched in anger. He'd bluffed and lost, but he didn't show it. He was once the best runner in New Vegas. He kept his poker face. "If that's what you want. I'll find my own way back. Don't worry about me; like you, I can take care of myself."

He left her at the conservatory and true to his word, he didn't look back once.

25

NAT CLOSED HER EYES SO THE TEARS wouldn't fall, pressed her lips together so she wouldn't call his name. She hadn't expected him to go, but he had. Was he just bluffing? That's probably what it was. He'd wanted her to stop him, to say something, anything to make him stay. But she'd just stood there, biting her lip while he walked away. *It's better this way.* This burden was her own, and if she was going to fulfill her destiny, she would have to stay focused. At least that's what she told herself. Half of her wanted to run after him. Half of her wanted to forget about whatever it was she was supposed to be doing. Hell, part of her just wanted to give up and collapse right there and then.

Call your drakon and it will come back to you, the Merlin had advised. Yes. She would do that—she'd come too far just to give up, though part of her wanted desperately to do just that. But too much was riding on what happened next. She told herself to get a grip, and to focus on the task ahead.

She closed her eyes, willing back the drakonsight. *Let me see once more through my drakon's eyes.* The Merlin had said her bond still existed—that it could not be broken. If it was there, buried somewhere within, she needed to find it, so she went back to the time when she last rode upon the drakon's back. *How did I feel when I rode upon the drakon?* She recalled the wind in her hair and the heat rising off the drakonflame. The thrill of diving through the sky. The heart-pounding exhilaration of victory. She remembered the way the creature trembled when it readied itself to breathe flame, the way the fire would churn within it. She could almost feel the wind on her face, the warm scales shifting beneath her legs.

At first she only saw what was in front of her, the glass conservatory of Apis, the rubble and the broken statues, the charred door.

But then she saw it again.

A second image, one of the skyline of New Dead City. Two images laid over each other. Two sets of eyes. A warm feeling stirred within her. She was back inside the head of Drakon Mainas. She knew the creature's thoughts, its urges, its fiery heart, and, this time, she knew Eliza's heart as well. Nat felt the weaver's desperation, her thirst for revenge. They were ugly feelings, but try as she might Nat couldn't shield herself from them. She felt the hatred, the confusion. She pitied Eliza. To live with such hate. She wondered how anyone could manage.

Eliza had bonded with the drakon, and now Nat would be bonded with both of them. It wasn't exactly what she'd wanted. Her head felt like a loud room, her thoughts were crowded, unclear, but Nat cut through the static. She cried out with her heart of dread.

Drakon Mainas, come back to me.

26

THE SPEAKING STONE TURNED HOT WHEN
he held it. *Where are you?* Wes sent. *Send coordinates.*

New Dead City, Shakes replied. *You guys out of the Red?*

Yeah.

You got the drak?

Not exactly.

Huh?

Wes, what is going on? Liannan's voice cut through like crystal. *Where are you? Where's Nat? Is everything all right?*

But before he could respond, the ground rumbled under his feet. *Godfreezeit. Hold on.* He put the speaking stone away and ran back to the conservatory, cursing himself for being as stubborn as Nat. He wasn't too proud to admit when he was wrong. He would happily eat his words if only it meant nothing had happened to Nat in the few minutes he had left her side. What had possessed him to leave her?

He skidded to a stop when he reached the glass chamber. The Great Conservatory of Apis was collapsing, its glass dome breaking, sending fatally sharp shards falling to the floor. One was headed right toward Nat, who was looking up at the ceiling, paralyzed.

"Nat! Above you!" he warned.

She didn't move, and so he made a flying leap and tackled her to the floor, rolling her to the side before it could hit her. The glass crashed a hairsbreadth away from where they lay.

"We need to get out of here," he said, breathing heavily from the effort and trying not to crush her body with his. "But I'm not sure I remember the way back to the surface."

"I don't think we have to take that route," she said, still pinned under him as she pointed to the glass dome above them.

A shadow passed across the glass, a great black beast, its wings stretched like two dark sails. Mainas.

"You called it back," he said, reluctantly disentangling his body from hers.

"Yes, but it's fighting me," she said, taking his hand this time when he offered it to help her stand. Neither of them mentioned the earlier spat or that Wes had returned. It seemed trivial once the enemy had appeared. "Where's Eliza? She doesn't seem to be riding it."

"Maybe Mainas got rid of her when you called it," he said hopefully, although he knew that was a pipe dream, as sweet as one of those violet cigarettes Shakes preferred.

"Maybe," said Nat, unsure.

Drakon Mainas's dark silhouette passed across the glass once more, its shadow growing larger. This time, it struck the glass with enough force to rattle the entire conservatory. A terrible wrenching sound shot throughout the chamber.

Its talons broke through the dome, sending more sheets of glass tumbling toward them. A mighty *crash* echoed through the conservatory. The drakon came again, its shadow visible through the cracks in the dome. It descended, turning in a great circle before laying its talons into the dome, rending the great curving iron beams that supported the glass, twisting them like twigs and tossing them aside. Above them, the ceiling collapsed in a shower of broken glass, metal, and stone.

Nat called to her drakon. She screamed its name as Wes grabbed her and raised his shield, so that the debris bounced harmlessly around them. The sound was maddening. Everywhere around them the glass was shattering upon the stones, but none of it touched them, not even the smallest piece.

"Thanks," she whispered, her head tucked under his chin.

"I shouldn't have left," he murmured, holding her close. "I won't ever again."

"I'm sorry, too," she whispered, so softly that he wondered if he had dreamed it.

There came a screech like a banshee's, and they looked up to see the black drakon hovering above them, blocking out the blue sky, circling.

Nat pulled away to scream at the monster. "Drakon Mainas!" she cried out again, but the monster gave no care.

The creature breathed fire so hot it melted steel and glass. Only Wes's power kept the flames at bay, keeping them safe. Arches collapsed and columns buckled. The ground tilted and threatened to give way. They rocked on their feet, holding close to each other for balance. It seemed as if the whole conservatory would be gone in a minute, and maybe all of Apis would be gone, too. The creature seemed bent on destroying everything it could lay its claws into.

The drakon burst through the remains of the dome. It roared and set the walls of the conservatory on fire. Everything crumbled into ash; the walls of the conservatory were collapsing. This was it, the end. They had no more time.

Nat called once more to her drakon. "Mainas!"

It twisted its neck toward her, then snorted, raking its claws on the shattered floor where it landed.

"Don't!" Wes said, holding her back.

"It won't harm me, it won't," said Nat. "It is mine."

The creature bent its neck, bowing low before her, as if daring her to come to its side. It looked as though it might tear her to pieces. It regarded her as if she were a stranger, but Wes knew she was no stranger to it. Eliza had only confused the drakon. She'd woven a web of illusions, and it was Nat's task to break that web. Wes knew about Eliza's power; he knew what Nat was up against and pitied her. This would not be easy.

Wes looked down at Nat, so small in his arms, and knew he had to let her go even though everything in his body and mind screamed he was insane to do so. With his heart in his throat, he released her and watched as Nat slowly picked her way toward her drakon.

For a moment, he thought it would relent, that it would dip its neck and accept its rydder, and Nat would be back where she belonged.

Until he saw, from the corner of his eye, a white fluttering atop the drakon's back. It was a corner of Eliza's white robe.

She had burrowed herself deep into its scales but now she appeared, triumphant and crazed.

"Nat! Stop!" he yelled.

Too late.

Eliza tugged on the reins she had fashioned around the drakon's neck, ugly iron chains that had melted into its hide.

"Burn her!"

27

NAT LOOKED STRAIGHT INTO THE drakon's gaping maw. There was a light at the end of it. Like a dim candle at the base of a deep well, the light flickered on and off. Then it grew brighter and Nat had the sensation of falling, tumbling toward that distant flickering. The dim flame grew brighter till suddenly it was no longer a candle. It was a bright and blistering sun. Drakon Mainas gave a tortured scream, shaking her out of her trance. Wes was yelling, stumbling as he ran to her; he hadn't had time to deflect the creature's attack, no time to send up his shield. She saw the drakonflame coming closer and steeled herself for the blast. The drakon exhaled. White-hot flame engulfed her, leaving her all alone, bathed in fire, trembling at the creature's might. The roar of the flame and the sheer intensity of its light blocked out everything else. For a moment Wes was gone, the drakon was gone. There was nothing but white light, surrounding her on all sides.

If she were anyone else, that light would be the last

thing she ever saw. For anyone else, the heat of the drakon-flame would mean death, the end. But Nat was no ordinary person—she was the rydder. The heat left no scars on her flesh, no blisters or burns. The white-hot light did not make her blink or cover her eyes, nor did she cover her ears to squelch the roar. She felt no pain, no discomfort of any kind. Like warm water in a bath, the flame caressed her skin, rejuvenating her.

Nat stretched out her arms and let her head fall back. A great gout of flame washed down upon her, and she did not shrink from it. She stood in the middle of the fire, letting the flames lick every part of her, so that it burned inside and out. *Don't worry*, she wanted to tell Wes. *There is nothing to fear*. The fire did not harm her—it restored her.

Each burst of flame made her feel stronger.

She heard a voice echo in her thoughts. *Is that you, Wes?* No. It wasn't Wes, but it was a familiar voice. It was garbled at first, faint, incomprehensible. She tried to ignore it, but it kept coming back, surrounding her like the flames.

Is that you, Mainas?

A powerful roar echoed in her thoughts.

The flame had not simply restored her strength. It had begun to mend the bond between drakon and rydder. Little by little the drakonflame was restoring their connection, slowly stitching their souls back together. The drakon exhaled once more, covering her in flame, and she heard its thoughts, clear as they had once been. Soon, she would be whole again.

When the flame faded, she was not only uninjured, she was

glowing with good health. She felt more alive, even stronger than before. The light was pouring from her, radiating from every inch of her body.

The feeling didn't last.

Eliza screamed her rage, pulling on the reins so that Mainas gnashed against the iron hooked around its mouth. With an angry shout, she shot back into the air, the drakon swooping and swerving without warning, attempting to throw her from it back. The drakon had two masters. Though Nat shared a link with her drakon, the creature was still bonded to Eliza.

From below, Nat could see the black drakon struggling, its wings flapping oddly, its muscles convulsing.

If Eliza couldn't have the drakon, she would destroy it, Nat saw, terrified for the creature.

Mainas, stop. Mainas, calm, she tried to send, but she fell backward as if she'd received a blow to the head.

SHE IS NOT YOUR RYDDER! Eliza sent. The shock of Eliza's strength sent her reeling. The warm glow faded from her skin.

Nat touched her face, felt blood dripping out of her ear, while Wes scanned the skies, alert for another assault.

"The bond—we have to break her bond with Mainas," Nat told him. "It's the only way."

"Can you bring them back?" asked Wes. "If you get them close, I can take care of Eliza."

"Are you sure?"

"Bring them here," he said. She knew he was remembering the fierceness of the creature he had first encountered on the

Pacific. It had nearly torn his ship to shreds, and it had tossed one of his crewmembers into the ocean, but he was not afraid. "Bring her to me. She is my sister. She is my responsibility."

Nat closed her eyes, focusing on her drakon once more.

The creature crashed through the hole again, plummeting to the floor, landing in a cloud of dust and dirt.

Nat and Wes ran toward it.

The drakon was bleeding from its iron chains, its eyes weeping red tears that matched Nat's own.

Without hesitation, Wes jumped on the drakon's back and pulled his sister down to the ground.

28

ELIZA SCRATCHED AND CLAWED AND kicked and threw herself across the room. The fire within her surprised Wes. Eliza would not give up easily. She wasn't his sister anymore; she was changed. She had taken so many lives and so much power, it had altered Eliza and made her into something terrible. Wes followed her, a terrible feeling building within him. This wouldn't end well.

He knew her tricks, what she would do. But her power surprised him nonetheless. Her life was on the line, so she gave him everything she had. The world went dark and Eliza vanished. In her place, Wes saw his sister as he had last seen her—on the night the Queen stole Eliza. He saw that little girl, looking frightened and alone. She called out to him. "Help me," she said. "Help me, Wes!"

He shook it off. Though it pained him, he ignored her illusion. *It's not real. She's not a little girl, and whatever innocence she had is gone.* Eliza was gone. He looked again at the little girl, and it did not break his heart. He saw only his sister's cruelty.

"Is this all you have, dear sister?" It was too late for her to play the innocent little girl, for she'd strayed from that path a long time ago.

Something struck him on the jaw and he tumbled backward. While he'd daydreamed, that little girl had attacked him, knocking him on the head with something heavy. *Not bad*, thought Wes. Maybe she hadn't wanted his sympathy. Maybe all she needed was a distraction, something to keep him busy while she slashed his throat, bashed in his brains. Wes glared at the little girl. She giggled a sickly little giggle as the illusion faded.

The baby girl was gone. Eliza stood in her place, her eyes flashing with anger.

I've got to strike before—

Too late, Eliza disappeared again. Now he saw only Nat, standing before her drakon. He watched in horror as the great black monster tore her limb from limb, rendering her body to pieces, blood splashed upon the stones.

No.

He dispelled the illusion, but she quickly made another.

He was on the battlefield and everyone was there, Shakes and Liannan. They were pinned down by soldiers. They were trapped. In a moment, they'd be done. The soldiers were surrounding them now, executing his friends while Wes watched.

No! No more illusions. He'd had enough. It was time to end this.

She hit him, lie after lie, but he shattered them all. He could break her illusions, but could he break the weaver who made them? Or was she just too strong? Had she taken too many lives and too much power?

How do I do this?

His magic was strong—he'd fought the Queen and triumphed—but Eliza was something different. Her power was equal to a hundred Queens. But then Wes remembered that magical energy was much like any other energy. The more you used it, the more it faded. When he'd first used his power, the magic had drained him to near death. Eliza was too strong to fight, but maybe he could drain her power. *Can I wear you down?*

"Is that all you've got?" he yelled, taunting his sister. Wes already afraid of what she might to do him next. If he goaded her into using all of her strength, she just might do it, and he shuddered to think what would happen when she did.

In answer, she sent a wave of energy that was so strong it knocked him off his feet, but instead of fighting the blow, he let it pass through him, absorbing and nullifying it. Wes couldn't use his magic to hurt others—he could only dissolve magic, so that was how he would fight her. Shock wave after shock wave rolled through him. He felt as if he were standing on the beach, holding his ground as wave after foaming wave washed over him, each one threatening to knock him down and drag him under. But he stood upright and absorbed her every blow. Eliza gave it all she had. After a time, she must have guessed at his strategy and known that he was wearing her down. Each time he absorbed her strength, it angered her and she poured even more power into her next attack.

She did not think he would triumph; perhaps that thought did not even occur to her. Over and over she attacked and he defended.

In the end, Eliza lasted longer than Wes thought she would.

He waited until her strength waned and he knew she was vulnerable. Then he reached for the slender thread that bound the creature to his sister. While Eliza was focused on destroying him, he found the bond between her and the drakon. He focused all of his power upon it.

And snapped it.

Eliza fell to the ground, lifeless.

Breaking the bond had doomed Eliza.

Wes had known what would happen when he shattered Eliza's magic. When he'd broken the Queen's spell, he'd knocked her out cold. He guessed something similar would happen to Eliza, but he hadn't thought it would kill her.

Wes knelt beside Eliza.

He remembered Emrys standing above the dead body of Nineveh, as he loomed over the broken form of his twin, conflicting emotions roiling inside—grief, regret, sorrow, anger. Eliza Wesson had brought so much damage to the world, but he found that at the last, the dominant feeling in his heart was one of compassion. She was a broken child of the ice, just like them. In a way, they were all shattered, all broken. Eliza had suffered more than most, but she'd done more harm, too. She had been stolen from her family, raised to think she was special. Her failure was their failure to love her for who she was. She'd never really had a family, a mother. The Queen had wanted to use Eliza. She was a pawn, a tool, a means to an end. And when that end was not achieved, when Eliza failed to enter the tower, it had destroyed her.

What kind of magic was this? What kind of magic demanded that a mother sacrifice her child? What kind of magic twisted its bearer into a monster?

Wes knelt by her side and took his sister into his embrace.

Eliza blinked her eyes at him. "Ryan?" she asked. "Where am I?" Her blue eyes were brown now, like his. This was the sister he'd known for a brief period, before her sixth birthday, before the corruption, before the darkness inside her had taken root and festered. When she was an innocent girl, still.

"You're with me," he said, brushing back her hair as the color drained from her face.

"I'm cold," she said.

"I'm sorry," he said, holding her up. "I'm so sorry, Eliza, I'm so sorry I couldn't protect you."

She stared at him. "But you did protect me. You took it away," she whispered.

"What?" he asked, unable to understand in his grief. That she would return to herself at the end was unexpected and searing.

"The dark thing inside me isn't there anymore," she whispered. Her eyes fluttered and rolled to the back of her head.

"But how?" he asked. When he'd hit her with all his strength, he must have done more than just knock her down. He had destroyed the dark magic within her, the rot that had driven her mad for all these years.

"Thank you," she said.

"No," he murmured. He couldn't lose her now, just when

he'd gotten her back. She was his sister again, the one he had tried to rescue. She was the girl he had hoped to find at MacArthur Med.

"Eliza, don't go," he said, pressing his hands to her heart, trying to make it beat again. He breathed air into her lungs, he did what he could, but it was no use. "Don't go," he said, but she was already gone.

Wes sagged under the dead weight. He closed her eyes with his fingers. The only family he had left was gone from this world.

Then he looked up. Somewhere, Nat was waiting for him, her drakon at her side. What remained of their crew—Shakes, Liannan, Brendon—needed them.

Family was what you made of it.

29

N AT WALKED TO THE SUFFERING CREATURE
and stroked its neck and removed the iron chains, letting
them clatter. *Easy,* she sent, soothing the drakon. *Easy. She is
gone. We are free.*

The drakon bowed and Nat walked to the place where
its shoulder met its neck. She nuzzled upon the creature's
shoulders. She was whole at last, bonded once more to the
creature, and she had Wes to thank for that.

"Eliza?" she asked when she saw Wes.

He shook his head.

"I'm sorry," she said, and she was. She knew that the loss
was a blow, no matter what kind of person Eliza had become.
She ached for him, for what he had had to do. He had killed
his own blood for her.

"She died in peace. She came back to me, in the end. She
wasn't . . . Lady Algeana anymore."

Nat nodded, knowing there were no words that would
make the grief easier, but she could offer comfort and

succor nonetheless. "Come," she said, opening her arms to him.

He fell into them, putting almost all of his weight on her, but she stood firm, holding him, wrapping her arms around him so that his grief flowed out and into her, so that they shared it, so that he knew that he was safe, that he was loved.

Her shoulder became wet with his tears, and she was crying as well. Eliza's was not the first death and would not be the last.

After a long silence, he rocked back on to his feet and pulled away slightly. "Is Mainas all right?"

"The drakon will heal."

"And you?"

"I can bear the pain."

"But you don't have to bear it alone," he said.

She was silent.

He put his arms around her once more and put his mouth next to her ear. "I was thinking about what Emrys said. About the sacrifice that's part of the spell," he said.

She tensed, wondering what he was going to say next. It was not what she expected.

"I know what it is," he said. "It's me. That's why you pushed me away. Because you thought you could make me leave you."

It appeared she was the only one who had been in denial about what the sacrifice entailed. "How long have you known?"

"When you stopped talking to me," he said. "I knew there had to be a good reason. And there could only be one reason for it. You're trying to keep me alive. Because you can't live a second without me."

"Cocky boy," she whispered, but she was smiling even as she said it.

He tightened his hold on her as the drakon lifted its wings and flapped toward the sky. "I wanted you to tell me yourself. But you really are stubborn. So I have no choice but to tell you now."

"Tell me what?" she asked, as they flew from the ruins, looking down on the devastated cityscape below.

"I'm not leaving you. Ever. I'm right here. Whatever that spell wants, whatever it needs, I'm here. If you die, I die with you. You're only trying to save me somehow and that's not going to work. We're in this together. I share your burden. I've seen the weight you carry. You can't do it alone."

Nat let the tears flow down her cheeks, letting the wind carry them. "But you'll die," she whispered, shaking in his arms.

Wes leaned even closer, so that his lips were against her wet cheek now, and he knew she was crying. "If that's what you need from me," he said.

"Ryan," she said. "I can't do it. I can't do it. I can't let you die. I won't." She was sobbing now, her shoulders shaking. "I wanted you to think I didn't love you, so you would leave me. But I love you so much. I can't let you go."

Wes kissed the tears as they fell. "You don't have to let go. You can't anyway. I'll be there till the end. Remember my promise? I'm never leaving you."

Even as they stood at the edge of the precipice, she felt a lightness and joy to know she wasn't alone. She had Mainas. She had Wes. Their friends were still alive and would help them secure the tower.

"I knew you never stopped loving me," he said, his voice as shaky as hers. She twisted around so that she faced him, raising her chin so that he leaned down and they shared a brief but sweet kiss.

"I'm sorry we wasted that time apart," she said.

"I'm sorry, too." He cleared his throat. "But there's no time to dwell on that now. I spoke to Shakes and Liannan. They've reached New Dead City. Avo's troops have surrounded the tower. They're going to blast it with nukes to try to get inside," he said.

"Let's go then." Nat lifted her foot, placed it upon the drakon's spine, and swung up onto its back. The scales felt warm beneath her, like coal rustling in a fire. The sound of the scales moving across one another was soothing, familiar. She was back where she belonged. She offered him her hand and he took it, swinging to sit behind her.

They flew away while, below, Apis gave one last sigh and collapsed completely. Its walls caved in, one after another, falling upon each other, shooting up towers of dust and sand that the drakon deftly avoided.

"I'm scared, Wes. I don't know what's going to happen, but I know it's not going to be good."

He murmured into her hair. "Emrys said there was always hope. I'm going to cling to it."

Hope was a thread as fine as drakonscale. Nat decided she would do the same.

RING AND TOWER

There they stood, ranged along the hill-sides, met
To view the last of me, a living frame
For one more picture! In a sheet of flame
I saw them and I knew them all. And yet
Dauntless the slug-horn to my lips I set,
And blew *Childe Roland to the Dark Tower came.*
—ROBERT BROWNING

Go then, there are other worlds than these.
—STEPHEN KING, *THE DARK TOWER, BOOK I: THE GUNSLINGER*

30

WHEN THE ICE CAME, THE COASTS WERE the first to fall. The waters rose, claiming the coastal lands, drenching the streets with black water, making the cities uninhabitable. New Dead City was devastated. The city that never slept entered a long hibernation. It forgot about its past. Names faded and the city became one more ruin in a world full of ruins. The Gray Tower was one of those ruins, those places that had lost their names. It was once called by another name, a building of the Empire State. This had been a great metropolis once, from the time before, a magnificent skyline of glistening towers of steel and glass. Its citizens fretted over what to eat and what to wear. They worried over luxuries. War had come to the city once before, leveling two of its marvelous towers to dust, but the city had recovered, had built new towers, more towers, until this one was just a tower in a city full of them. Now those towers were rotted. Some were collapsed; none stood intact. Though broken in places, the Gray Tower stood above the rest. Almost everything around it had fallen, making it appear as if the tower were some last holdout against the end of the world. It looked as if it were waiting, holding on until someone arrived to claim the power within it.

In the dead of the night, Wes and Nat came to the city. In a swirling cloud of energy, they appeared above the dark waters of the Atlantic. They were perched atop the drakon's back, clinging to each other. There were only a few passages that connected the Gray Lands to Vallonis, but a door from Vallonis could take you anywhere in the Gray Lands. So they had used one such door to bring them here, to the doorstep of the tower.

Wes had half expected to see a few lights in New Dead City or a fire burning behind a broken window, but the city was quiet, dead like its name. The once-glittering towers were caked in soot and grime. The streets that had glowed with light were now dark. Only the snow and ice gave off the occasional shimmer.

Shakes had told them to meet on the sixteenth floor of a building twenty streets south of the Gray Tower. Wes saw the great tower and counted the dark streets till he found the one Shakes had identified. Its sign read MANHATTAN PENTHOUSE. They circled once in the darkness, looking for a place to land, but found none. Even if they could land here, there was nowhere to hide the drakon, so Mainas took them to an edge of the city where they left him in an abandoned warehouse. Wes and Nat made their way back on foot, navigating the streets, bounding over piles of snow and ice, dodging the broken cars that hid within the piles of white.

Through a great hole in one of its walls, they slipped inside and on the sixteenth floor, they found a broken window that let them keep watch on the streets below while they waited for Shakes to arrive.

An hour passed, maybe two, and the sky turned a deep shade of purple. Wes motioned to Nat when saw signs of movement in the distance.

"Do you see them?" she asked, joining him at the window.

There was movement in the street corner below, three shapes flitting between the shadows.

"I think so," he said, pointing. "Isn't that Brendon?" The smallman zigzagged through a street full of rusted taxicabs. Shakes was next, then Liannan.

After a few minutes, they heard the clatter of footsteps up the stairway and the door opened.

Brendon was the first to reach them. He was winded and out of breath, but still had a grin on his face.

Wes was glad to see the smallman happy.

"Mainas?" Brendon asked as he reached Wes and Nat.

Wes nodded, yes. Nat had got her drakon back. It would be ready to fight when the time came.

"Close by," said Nat. "Don't worry."

Wes gave Brendon a warm slap on the shoulder as Liannan and Shakes appeared in the doorway. There were both dressed in rags. They had posed as homeless marauders, hiding among the gangs that still populated the devastated city.

After the greetings and the hugs, and a chance for everyone to shake off the snow, Shakes led them to the makeshift war room and Liannan unrolled the map.

It was a map of the old underground railway, the subway, it was called.

There were lines drawn on the map in various colors. Each one represented a train line and the tunnel it traveled. The green and the yellow lines ran closest to the tower.

"They've blocked the green line," said Liannan. "They're using it to house troops and supplies, but the yellow is open. We'll enter at the station here." She pointed to a spot she had already circled. "We will follow the tunnel to here." She indicated a second spot, higher up on the map. "The road collapsed at this intersection, exposing the tracks to the sky," she said, pointing to the place where the yellow line intersected a street named Thirty-Third. "We can climb out of the underground here to avoid the checkpoint they've set up at the street named Thirty-Fourth."

"So the street names are all numbers?" asked Shakes jokingly. "Guess they weren't too creative back then."

"Great input, Shakes." Wes shook his head. "Any other little gems you can share with us?"

"Just trying to liven things up. Life's been a bit dreary lately."

"Can I continue?" Liannan asked, as she gave Shakes a glare that made the boy shut his mouth.

"Keep going, Liannan," Wes said. "Tell us about the army."

"We tracked them to here," Liannan said, pointing to the east side of the map. She was talking about Avo's soldiers. "They were launching missiles at Eliza as she flew toward the tower. We were sure the drakon would set the tower afire, but at the last moment, it turned away and disappeared."

"I called it to me," said Nat with a smile.

"Just in time; she was about to roast us," Shakes said with a smile.

"What about Avo?" asked Wes.

"Yeah, that icehole's here. But he can't get inside. The mist is impenetrable. We think he's going to nuke the place as soon as his drones get their new warheads," said Shakes. "We saw some technicians refitting the drones for what we guessed were nukes."

"So while we have time, we need to hit it. Tomorrow we'll take a team over here," Liannan said, pointing to a place on the east side of the tower, far away from the subway line at the street called Thirty-Third. "Draw their fire, distract them while a small strike team heads up to the tower without any-one noticing. Before Avo destroys everything."

"Strike team?" Nat asked.

"Me and Wes," said Brendon proudly.

"Seriously?" Wes looked sideways at the smallman. "I didn't know you were 'strike team' material."

"Oh, I don't plan on fighting, that's your job. I'll open the doors, but you'll have to do the rest." Brendon said, his fists raised in a boxer's stance.

Wes shrugged. He knew what Brendon meant when he said, "You'll have to do the rest." Wes would need to take on the tower's magic—the mist or whatever it was—that had held back Eliza. He would need to defeat the tower's magic. The thought made his stomach churn. He would have to succeed where she had failed. Eliza was stronger than all of them put together, but the tower had defeated her. *How much hope do I have?*

"Anything else?" Nat asked.

"There's a few details, but we can go over those later," Liannan said. "I think Shakes here is going to tear his hair out if we don't give him something to eat."

There was a tin can, half rusted, balanced above a fire. Brendon was cooking. Warm smoke drifted up from the flames. Black beans. Not his favorite, not even close to a pizza squeezer, but at least they would eat. Shakes held Liannan. Nat sat close to Wes. Everyone was quiet at first, maybe a little nervous. The air held an edge. Would this be the last time they would all sit together? No one wanted to say it, but Wes gathered that everyone felt the same way. No one wanted to say good-bye. Couldn't they all just stay here like this? Warm and together?

Brendon pulled the can from the fire and everyone shared what was in it. Liannan sang a song; Shakes looked at her, dreamy. Her voice echoed in the open space, filling the air with its warmth. Shakes hummed along. In between choruses Liannan talked about their wedding, what she would wear and how they would say their vows. She spoke at length about the sylph culture and the simple vows they exchanged, the handmade rings. Shakes nodded quietly. There was pain on his face. The more she said, the more it hurt, Wes knew. It wasn't that he didn't want a wedding. It was that Shakes finally knew it was just a fantasy. They would never make it to that wedding. None of them would.

Especially since Nat did not deny what he had guessed about the spell and the sacrifice. They would not survive the morrow.

"Come on," Nat said, taking his hand. "It's late."

"Where are we going?" he asked.

She showed him.

The building they had camped in was an old hotel, a grand one, and after the ice some of the rooms were still intact. She opened the door to a suite that rivaled New Vegas's best high-roller palaces. The room had two levels and curtains that stretched from floor to ceiling, marble floors that were as black as night. Tall glasses and a bottle of wine waited on a table next the door, looking expectant, as if someone had anticipated their arrival.

Maybe someone had.

Brendon, Wes thought, *it had to be.*

Wes closed the door behind him, and watched as she walked over to the bed and began to unbutton her jacket. He did the same and removed his shoes and socks, tossed them to the side. But when Nat began to hitch her shirt up he shook his head and walked over.

He stood in front of her. "Let me," he said. He wanted to tell her he'd been dreaming of this moment. "You know, Nat . . . it isn't just Shakes who wants a wedding." He had dreams for them, too. He was going to save up for a ring. He was going to ask her to be his.

"I'm already yours," she whispered, as if she had read his mind. "There is no need to ask."

He helped her out of her shirt, out of her camisole, and she did the same, unbuttoning his shirt so that they were both bare in the moonlight.

"You're so beautiful," he whispered, tentatively putting a hand on her skin.

"So are you," she said, her hands fluttering over his chest, skimming over the muscles in his torso, making his breath catch. Fire, her touch was fire.

"I wanted you the minute I saw you in the casino, even when you stole my chips," he murmured, tracing a line from her neck to her chest, and growled when she trembled under his hand in response.

They fell to the bed, and he bent over her, a hand on her belt, tugging. "Is this okay?" he asked. "Are you sure?"

In answer, she wrapped her hand around his, helped him unbuckle and undress her some more. Then she leaned over and did the same to him, pulling off his belt with a smile. She pulled him down to her, and he followed eagerly as they kissed. When she rolled her tongue and bit his lip, teasing him, he found he couldn't hold back any longer.

Their bodies joined together, her hands running down his back, her legs entwined over his, and they moved in a rhythm that started sweet and slow and built steadily until they were both frantic and breathless; and when she screamed her joy, he covered his mouth with hers, every sense of his afire until he, too, was crying her name and shaking in her arms.

They would not have tomorrow, but they would have tonight, they would have this.

Wes thanked whatever luck he had that he had lived to this day.

31

I DON'T WANT THIS TO END. THIS *cannot be the end of us,* she thought, lying in his arms, his forearm circling around so that it pressed against her chest, her back to his front, his entire body covering hers as they curled like spoons. The dark gray of night had become the cool gray of morning.

"You're awake," he said, letting his hand wander over her skin, slowly stroking her side, his touch gentle, sending sparks all over.

She turned around to smile at him, feeling the shift in his body. "Again?" she teased. They had hardly slept the night, spending the hours exploring each other, until they knew every secret sound, every source of pleasure. She was sore and fulfilled, and ached from the loss that she would soon bear.

He was going to die today because of her.

"Don't think about it," he said, noticing the change in her, the tension in her shoulders. "Don't think."

Wes was right. In a few hours they would go to the Gray

Tower. If she was successful, she would cast the spell, which meant saying good-bye to him forever.

But he was here now.

She kissed his hand and he rolled her over so that she was on top of him, looking down. As she bent over him, her long dark hair fell on his face, on his chest.

He gazed at her through half-lidded eyes, his brown hair messy and his cheek dotted with stubble. "Nat," he said, sighing, as she continued to torment him, letting her hair tickle his cheek, driving him to madness, until he was fully awake now, and panting. "My Nat."

"Good morning," she whispered, and when she pressed her body down upon his, she was thrilled to find he was as ready and eager as she was.

He grunted, lifted her hips with his strong hands, and when she crashed down, he was there. But he took his time, rocking her gently, his eyes locked on hers, relishing in the moment, until they were breathless.

She dressed slowly, wanting to lengthen the time they had alone together as much as she could. He did the same and together they silently put on each item of clothing they had quickly discarded the night before. One sock after the other. Buttoning shirts. Pulling on pants. Buckling belts. Her sword. His rifle.

She pulled his jacket lapels together, giving it a crisp once-over, brushed the lint off his shoulders.

He smoothed her hair, tucking a stray strand behind her ear.

Outside the door, Brendon was already waiting. The small-man would lead them through the ductwork and hidden tunnels that led to the top of the tower without Avo and his soldiers noticing.

Shakes and Liannan would distract Avo, luring him away from the tower to fight them. If they got in trouble, she would send Mainas to help them, directing its flame.

"You'll do great," said Wes. "Let's do this."

Nat squared her shoulders, touched the charm around her neck for luck, and kissed him for the last time.

32

FOR A MOMENT WES THOUGHT THEY would make it, that the plan wouldn't fail and that they would be lucky for once. But once things went wrong, everything went wrong, and there was no way to make it right, there was only moving forward and through, no stopping the inevitable.

Brendon had led them, deftly unlocking doors with the same skill he'd shown when they lived in New Vegas, half a lifetime ago. He navigated the dark corridors and stairs, finding passages where Wes saw only darkness. Nat held Wes's hand, hurrying alongside him.

The tower had long ago been hollowed out and rebuilt from within. In places, he saw what must have once been offices: empty rooms, moldy desks, and piles of shredded paper. In the past century a new structure was built within the old. Blocks of stone concealed office walls. Wood doors bound in iron replaced the old metal ones. And granite blocks formed passages that narrowed to a width so slender Wes had to suck air through his teeth to pass. More than once he and Nat were forced to crawl on their knees. Everywhere, they found barriers, doors bound in iron and secured with heavy locks.

Every time, Brendon figured out how to open it.

Coming around a corner, Wes found Brendon, balancing on the tips of his toes as he fiddled with a lock.

Wes felt a bead of sweat run down his forehead. He exchanged an anxious look with Nat.

"He's got this one. You've got it, right, Donnie?"

Brendon grunted, and with a final push, the lock clicked into place and the door swung open. More corridors beyond, more passages and doors.

The Gray Tower was a vertical maze; Wes wondered whether they would ever find the top.

He stretched out both hands, touching each wall as he made his way forward. "Stay beside me," he said, bumping against Nat, feeling her warmth, enjoying the flash of memory from that morning.

But she slipped ahead of him, focused on her goal. He tried to follow the sound of her footsteps. "Wait up," he said, hoping they might slow down a bit.

Soon, he could no longer hear their footfalls.

"I'm just ahead," replied Brendon.

Nat said, "Watch the turn—"

What turn? Wes thought, trying to catch up. Then he slammed into a wall. *Oh, that turn.*

He rubbed his head. Her warning came too early.

In the darkness, he felt Nat's fingers wrap around his. She led him forward. "Sorry, I didn't realize you were so far behind," she whispered.

He knew what she was doing. Letting go. Saying good-bye.

Not yet.

Not yet.

They were still alive after all.

Brendon was up ahead, his shoes clanging against what must be a metal stairway. Holes in the wall admitted dim shafts of light, allowing Wes to catch sight of the smallman.

"This must be an old fire shaft," Brendon said, when they'd caught up to him. The metal stairs were rotted and the concrete crumbled. At best, half the steps were usable.

"You may want to be careful . . . ," he said, nodding toward the steps.

"Got that," said Wes, his foot resting anxiously on the rusting metal. Nat was already climbing. The smallman leapt ahead, the stairway creaking each time his foot met the tread. Wes held on to the rail, trying to spread out his weight. He thought he heard a noise behind him, but he couldn't be certain. Maybe it was nothing. He hoped it was nothing.

He peered through one of the holes in the wall and tried to gauge their elevation. "I figure we're past halfway up, maybe two-thirds," he said.

"Maybe higher," said Nat, looking over his shoulder.

"I guessed as much," Brendon said, his tools pressed into a lock at the top of the next flight.

"Maybe we should start locking these doors behind us— thought I heard footsteps . . . something."

Brendon paused, cocking his ear to the sky, listening.

"This whole tower is moaning."

"Like it's collapsing."

Wes looked around at the patchwork of construction. "From the sound of it, soon. Come on, we should hurry." He motioned to the next passage.

Another corridor led to a tall stairway. The wind whistled through cracks in the walls, and Wes knew they were higher now, closer to the top. The quality of the construction improved considerably on the upper floors. The walls were more smoothly carved, most likely kept intact by the magic of the Gray Tower.

"I think we're almost there," Wes guessed.

Brendon was already working on the next lock.

The sound of hard rubber hitting concrete echoed through the shaft. Wes spun, looked around, but didn't see anything. Brendon was still focused on the lock. Wes backtracked. Something was wrong. That noise. They weren't alone.

Footsteps. Coming closer. *Tap. Tap. Tap.*

They were being followed.

Ice.

The lock clicked open, the door at the top of the stairs swung wide. The passage beyond was different from the rest.

They had made it to the top.

Except they weren't alone.

"I'll hold them," said Brendon, reaching for his gun. "You and Nat go."

There was no time to argue, and Wes hurried back to Nat, pulling her up toward the stairs, just as the gunfire erupted. Shots ricocheted through the shaft. Sparks filled the air. A slab of concrete broke loose, striking the stairs below it, carrying down two or three treads and a piece of the rail.

When he reached the final door, Wes's fingers intertwined with hers and he drew her tightly against him. More shots. A bullet grazed his shoulder, tearing the fabric of his shirt but missing the flesh. It struck the wall with a mighty crack. His ears rang.

Nat removed the gray key she wore around her neck. It trembled in her fingers. She inserted it in the final lock, but it slipped from her grip. Wes caught the key and helped her press it back into the lock.

More shots, growing louder.

The key clicked into place. The lock spun.

There was a slight sucking of air as the door opened by narrow degrees.

Past the threshold, the mist was thick as cotton, but hard as rock. Wes tried to enter, tried to force his way through the haze, but could not. The magic held. There was no way inside.

This was what his sister had failed to do, had failed to achieve.

The battle drew closer. A strangled cry echoed behind him, and his stomach dropped. He knew what that was. Wes looked over his shoulder, just in time to see Brendon take a bullet and fall to the ground. Blood poured from the wound, drenching the steps, puddling around the smallman's slender form. Nat screamed, and Wes choked down a grunt, his gut groaning with anger, his body charged with anxiety.

Wes watched the light fade from Brendon's eyes, saw them go gray and narrow. *Donnie,* he thought. *Brave Donnie is with Roark now.* A second bullet hit his friend's dead body, making it twitch as if it were still alive. The sound of the bullet hitting the body made him shudder. Wes felt as if he had been the one who was shot, that he, too, would soon join the ranks of the dead.

The clank of boots on steel echoed from the stairs. A figure stopped alongside Brendon's body. His face was in shadow, until he looked up.

Avo Hubik.

He waved from the platform below with a demonic smile.

Wes turned to run down the steps, to protect Brendon's body, to take his revenge. Even if it meant losing his life, he'd risk it for the chance to strike back.

"No," Nat said. She must've known what was in his thoughts. "Wes, it's—"

"Too late. I don't care," he said and once more moved toward Avo. That heavy feeling in his stomach was growing, weighing him down. Sorrow hung above him like a great cloud, threatening to obscure everything around him. He needed to do something, now.

"Yes, you do care," she said. Nat put herself between Wes and the stairs. "You know this isn't the way, this isn't how we win."

He listened, and somehow he knew she was right. There was another way, another path. Avo would have his time, but this was not it. He'd come back for the drau. For now, he had to get Nat inside the tower.

Without saying anything, Wes relented; he turned and faced the open doorway and the mist. This was his task. He was meant to do this so Nat could cast the spell.

Wes pressed his hands against the mist. It was like brick, it was immovable.

"Can you hold back Avo?" he asked Nat, his words heavy with grief.

"I'll do my best," Nat said. Her voice was quiet, and she faced Avo boldly.

A moment later, a great crunching sound shot through the stairway, the sound of steel ripping and concrete shattering. It made his ears ring and he nearly lost balance when the building trembled. He glanced back at Nat and saw her silhouette bathed in flame. She must have poured all of her grief into a single attack, a white-hot rush of flame that had torn through the side of the building, rending steel and stone. She'd bought Wes the time he needed.

Turning to face the open door, he stabbed his fingers into the mist and pushed against it. He forced both arms into the gray cloud and entered. Immediately, the toxic haze assaulted his senses. The vapor reeked of copper and aluminum, a sickly tang that made his eyes water and his throat burn. The mist was more than a barrier—it was poison. Linger too long and it would consume him, burning him from within as he inhaled it. He took one step, then another. Soon the gray haze was all around him.

Hurry, he thought. *Hurry, before something happens to Nat, hurry before you're too weak to fight the magic.* Eliza had once come to this place. She had stood at this door and tried to dispel the magic within. She'd come here and failed. The significance was not lost on him. Eliza had always been the one with the gifts, the kid with all the power. If she had failed, how could he succeed?

Shut up, he told himself. *Shut up and focus.* There was no time to worry.

While he'd deliberated, the sickly haze had curled around his fingers and arms, drifting into his mouth and nose. He felt something warm at his back. Nat.

"Avo?" he asked.

"I've bought us some time," she said, her back pressing against his. He felt her shudder when the mist enveloped her.

"What's happening?" she asked.

"I don't know," he said. "Just hold on. I'm dealing with it."

He hoped he could deal with it. Wes again focused on the mist. Eliza must have fled; she must have run down the steps to avoid the poison, to keep it from saturating her every pore. Wes would not run—it was too late for that. He pressed deeper into the gray haze, pulling Nat alongside him.

You are nothing. He inhaled.

An illusion.

A trick of the light.

A test.

You will bend to me.

And open to my will.

The mist burned in his lungs. He felt it in his eyes.

Would it blind him?

"Wes!" Nat called through the gray. Her back pressed a little harder against his, the dull beating of her heart thudding against his skin. For a moment he worried the beat was slowing.

Bend. Begone.

I am the master here.

He breathed in the mist and understood that it was only an illusion. A trick. Like the ones Eliza had made as a child.

Wes had always known how to dispel illusions.

He yelled curses as he threw his strength against the mist.

They quarreled. His magic against the tower's.

The contest was a rout.

The haze shattered into pieces.

In one great exhalation it flew from the chamber, vanishing like a breath of steam.

It was done, the barrier shattered. They were in.

Wes pushed Nat inside the room.

"Wait!" she cried.

He shook his head. This was it. This was good-bye. This was the last time they would see each other. He knew it in his heart.

"Wes!"

"Good-bye, Nat," he said, and slammed the door behind her. When he turned around, he was ready to face his enemy and meet his death.

33

THE IMAGE OF BRENDON CRUMPLING TO the ground lingered in her thoughts. It followed her like a shadow. Nat could see the red spot spreading across the floor, and the smell of blood soiled her nose. She had wanted to bring the whole stairway down upon Avo, maybe even the whole building, but the mist had gotten into her eyes and her mouth, distracting her as Avo slipped away. She'd have gone after him if Wes hadn't pushed her into the tower before ducking back to deal with Avo.

"Wes!" she cried out but he was already gone, behind the door that had sealed shut.

"Good-bye, Nat."

"NO!"

But it was too late. He had closed the door. She was inside and he was on the other side of it.

But where was she? What was this?

What was that noise?

The sound of coins striking a metal tray echoed in the distance. She heard the spinning, twirling sound of a wheel, the unmistakable ring of slot machines, and the cry of a dealer calling out, "Blackjack!" The room was still dark, but now she saw twinkling lights slowly coming into focus. A buzzer rang out, the sound of dice rattling in a cup. There were shouts, too. The sound of gunfire and men yelling out orders.

I am in New Vegas. It didn't make any sense.

Somehow, she was back in the casino in New Vegas. Except everything was different. Chaos reigned. People were looting outside, stealing from the casinos, darkness inside and out.

"What happened?" she asked.

"The RSA is gone," said a dealer. "They sent all their soldiers to some distant battle in the East."

Why was she here?

Where was the *Archimedes Palimpsest*?

Why did the Gray Tower send her here?

A girl slammed into Nat, nearly knocking her to the ground. Nat stood, spun in a circle, taking in the scene. People were grabbing up piles of casino chips and knocking over slot machines, trying to get at the coins inside. Security had fled the room, and the pit bosses were nowhere to be seen. A few dealers huddled in the distance.

Past the chaos and the looting, through broken windows, she caught sight of the place where a glass bridge had once connected this casino to another. The bridge was gone; there was nothing but air between the towers.

The scroll is in that other tower, she knew.

But how would she get there? Below, the street teemed with rioters, with gunshots and men wielding clubs. There was blood on the ground and bodies. The lower floors of the other tower were wreathed in flames. Soon there would be little left of the tower, just another burned-out skeleton. Time to act. But how? *How do I reach the other tower?*

She stood at the window, staring at the gap between the buildings, at the place where the bridge had once stood.

She must take a leap of faith. The same one that she failed on her journey to Apis. She knew what to do. The knowledge was in her, had always been in her. Only now it had come to her like some long-lost relic unearthed along a familiar path.

Nat stared down at the teeming crowd below. Like ants they twisted and scattered, swarming over the streets. She hesitated, then remembered the words of her teacher, of Faix, who had sent her on this quest, to fix what had been broken. The memory came to her like a beacon in the dark, appearing in her thoughts just as she needed it.

One last test.

She walked to the edge of the window and stepped out into the air, her foot dangling above the nothingness. She had been here before—she wasn't scared. The wind blew in her face, the night was cold, and she embraced it. She gathered the air, harnessing its strength, forging the mighty wind into a new and solid form.

She reached out with her toe and touched a solid mass. She looked down. Funnels of air swirled beneath her, forming hazy towers of air. She had created a bridge out of ether. Something from nothing.

She ran across, sprinting through the sky. What a glorious sight it must have been: a girl dashing through the air as whirlwinds met her every footfall. The sky itself obeyed her commands. It whipped at her feet and at her back, the wind roaring at her like some petulant child, upset that she had forced it to bend to her will. She made one leap after another, carrying herself to the next building.

There was no door into the next tower, so she made one.

She made the glass bend and shatter, tearing a great hole in the wall. She leapt through the opening, towers of air escorting her, landing her smoothly on the floor in the casino.

In the middle of the room, a vid screen flashed on a jackpot machine.

Was this it?

It had to be.

She reached out toward the flashing light and everything disappeared.

34

WES TURNED TO AVO AS THE DOOR TO THE
tower shut with a bang. "What up, icehole," he greeted.

"Open the door," Avo said. "Let me in."

"Yeah, right. Maybe I can give you the scroll, too."

"Keep joking, Wesson," said Avo. He sounded smug, overly
confident, as if he knew something Wes did not. "Show him."

Two soldiers brought out Shakes and Liannan, captured
and chained. The distraction had worked, except for the escape plan.

"Open the door."

"Don't!" said Liannan.

Shakes bowed his head. "Well, boss, I guess this is
good-bye."

Wes scratched his chin. He wasn't done—not yet. *I won't
let it end like this.* His back was against the door, which was
cold and solid. There was no way Avo could get past it. Without the key and without Wes to part the mist, he would never
be able to enter the room.

"Open the door and do your thing," Avo said, his voice

raised. He was shaking. His hands were wet with perspiration. The stairs beneath him let loose a long moan, threatening to collapse.

"Careful, or this whole place will fall down and then you'll never get through."

"Doubt if you'd let that happen," Avo said, cocking the gun and holding it to Shakes's temple.

Would he do it?

Wes met his gaze. Avo grinned.

The drau was dead serious. He'd pull the trigger if Wes resisted. He'd shoot Shakes and Liannan, too.

"Open it!" Avo said, his finger itching. "I don't bluff. You know that, Wesson."

Wes knew as much. Avo had tried to kill him at least once, maybe twice. His past was all a blur.

"If I open that door, you'll still shoot," Wes said, thinking aloud, letting Avo know that he understood what was about to happen. His friends' futures were already written. Wes saw that. In these last moments he knew how everything would go down.

Avo's trigger finger tensed, and Wes lunged for the weapon. He couldn't let it end like this. *I won't stand and watch my friends die.*

His hand wrapped the barrel of the gun. Avo didn't hesitate. The weapon discharged, but the bullet went wide, striking a wall. The flash of the barrel blinded Wes, and the sound made his ears ring.

It all happened in the space of a breath: Avo tumbled to the floor, Wes on top of him, while Shakes struggled against the soldiers who held him. Avo still held the gun. He used it as a cudgel. He pounded the grip against Wes's skull, hit him twice, then took aim at Shakes. Wes was still on top and when he saw Avo aim the gun, he put his fist over the barrel, as if his own flesh would somehow stop the bullet. Something about the gesture made Avo pause, and when he did, Wes tore the gun from Avo's grip, tossing it to the floor.

I can do this, thought Wes. *I can still save everyone.* He knocked Avo twice on the jaw, hard enough to stun him, to leave him shaking and dizzy. Wes stood. Now he had to deal with the others.

This will work, he thought, but too late, he heard another shot ring out. It wasn't Avo; his gun lay on the floor.

There was another soldier with another gun.

A second shot rang like thunder in the shaft, the muzzle fire flashing like a bolt of lightning in the dark. There was blood on the stairs and Shakes lay lifeless at Avo's feet.

No! He lunged for the fallen body. But what could he do? The bullet had already ended him.

When the body had hit the stairs, it made a thud that Wes would never forget.

It folded like wet clay.

Liannan's mouth was open in grief, but her grief was beyond sound.

Avo brushed the dirt from his uniform and retrieved his lost pistol. He cocked the trigger and aimed.

Wes spied something heavy on the ground, a piece of metal attached to some glass, still burning from Nat's flame. He flung it at Avo, then threw himself at the nearest soldier. He never touched the man. The third soldier hit Wes on the head with something heavy. Wes stumbled backward, momentarily distracted, his vision blurry. He shook his head and cleared his vision. Startling the soldier beside him, Wes struck the man in the chest with a pair of swift blows. Then he turned and knocked the gun out of the hand of the other soldier. He moved so quickly there was no time for thought. He was just reacting, doing what he needed to do to save his friend. But it wasn't enough. There was nothing he could do to win.

Wes caught sight of the drau, one hand wrapped around Liannan's neck, the gun put to her head.

"You know what'll happen next," Avo said. Even the drau sounded disgusted. This was dirty business. All of this was wrong.

"Let her go," Wes said. "It's not worth it, Avo." Wes's voice was quiet. He was saving his energy, buying time. He knew what would come next, but he still couldn't accept it. He had to keep trying. Maybe there was some magic that could bring back Shakes. He told himself to keep trying, that there was always another way.

Wes found something hard, a piece of fractured concrete, a bit of the wall that had come loose.

He hurled it at Avo's skull.

A shot rang out at the same time. The rock struck the drau just as the bullet left the chamber. Avo yelled.

But the shot had already been fired.

The target hit.

Liannan crumpled to the ground next to Shakes.

The two of them together, motionless. Forever.

Wes's stomach sank to his knees, his entire body shivering, his brain not believing what his eyes showed him. He knew this was the end, but the sight of it hurt more than any bullet.

There is another way, he told himself. *Enter the tower, part the gray mist, find the scroll. There is another way,* he told himself again and again, to make the pain go away. It was the only way he could keep going. *We'll fix this. In the end we'll fix everything.* But even he didn't believe that. There was hardly anyone left to do any fixing.

Farouk. Roark. Eliza. Brendon. Shakes. Liannan.

I'm next.

"Open the door. Or it's your turn," Avo said, bleeding from where the rock had struck him, picking up the gun, aiming it at Wes.

"I'm not afraid of death," said Wes. He hurt so much he could barely talk. His head was pounding, thudding like a hundred hammers. But he was lying. *I am afraid,* he thought. Mostly he was afraid of Nat dying.

There were three of them and only one of him.

The building shook, and a distant sound echoed through the holes in the walls.

"Open the door, Wesson. There is no sense in fighting. You are unarmed and outmanned."

Wes shook his head. He'd never open that door.

The look on his face must have been easy to read. Avo's grin flattened and he gritted his teeth. "We both know you are going to die, but if you open that door I'll do it quickly, a bullet to the head and it'll be over. Otherwise, we'll take our time with you. After a day or two you'll beg us to let you open that door."

Wes didn't listen. The words didn't register. He would never let Avo pass through the door. "Why? If you knew what you were, why?" Wes asked. "Why did you slaughter your own kind?"

"Why not? One hundred and eleven years I've lived on the gray side. Cast out, abandoned."

"Your mother did it to save you."

"My mother is a whore."

"Your words, not mine," said Wes. "Though it does give me an idea. I hadn't thought of it until now, but the two of you are a lot alike."

"Spare me your observations, Wesson."

"Well, I was there when she passed. I saw the way she lived and the way she died."

"The Queen is dead?" he asked. Avo almost sounded as like he had a heart. "Good. I'm glad someone ended it."

"I ended it," said Wes. "I was the one who broke her, just as I'm the one who'll break you."

"Well, you're half right, Wesson."

A far-off sound drifted through a crack in the wall, the sound of beating wings coming closer. The floor beneath him rattled, the dust stirring on the floor. *What's happening?*

A moment before the creature struck, Wes recognized the pounding of the drakon's wings. He heard the familiar sounds of the creature and ducked for cover, hiding among the debris. A moment later, a cloud of flame tore through the tower's walls. The drakon broke through glass and stone, rending an opening in the stairwell. Avo's soldiers cowered before the beast, then tried to find cover, but it was too late—the drakon was upon them. It reached into the building, gathering up the soldiers with its talons and taking them away.

Wes watched the creature go. It had taken the soldiers and gone, eliminating the threat to the rydder.

The tower was safe.

He brushed the soot from his jacket and face and breathed deeply, mentally thanking Nat and her drakon.

The moment didn't last.

"I'm glad I saw you duck for cover," said Avo as he climbed from the remains of the stairway. "When I saw you hide, I did the same. I guess my grunts weren't quite as clever."

"Only an icehole like you would leave his men to die."

"I'm not a hero, Wes."

"No one ever said you were," Wes said. He looked Avo and down. The drau had no weapon. He must have lost it in the scuffle. "Noticed you don't have a gun aimed at my head. I guess it's just you and me now. No more guns and knives."

"Suits me," said Avo. "Guns make killing easy. I like to do it with my hands," he said.

"Works for me," said Wes as the two circled. The stairwell was open to the sky. The drakon had torn a massive, smoking hole in the side of the building. There were stray fires all around them and smoke filled the air, all of it pouring out into the sky. If Wes stepped to his left he'd tumble off the edge, and if he went left he'd run into a wall of flame. There was nowhere to go, no way to escape. It was just the two of them, alone on a platform in the sky, the building below them threatening to collapse, the air filled with the stink of drakonfire. He'd hoped the drakon would return, but the air was quiet, the sky empty.

Wes's sights narrowed to a slit and he saw only Avo. There was nothing else. No tower. No stairs. It was just Wes and Avo.

Avo's mark was shining. There was blood on his chin where the concrete struck him.

"Let's end this," Wes said.

35

THE JACKPOT MACHINE—THE *ARCHIMEDES*
Palimpsest—came to life. Each turn of the wheel revealed another line of the spell, one after another, as if Nat were unroll-
ing a great scroll. Her face lit by the glow of the machine, she
memorized the lines, taking each into her thoughts. She was
in a casino—lights flashed and machines tinkled all around
her—but she ignored it all. She heard nothing; she saw only
the words.

There was a stool attached to the machine and she sat on it.
She placed both hands in her lap and forgot about the world
around her. She forgot she once worked in a casino, that she'd
spent her days shuffling cards and exchanging banter with the
clients. She forgot about her drakon and the war she'd fought.
Nothing that came before this moment mattered. *This is what
I am here to do.* The bright letters revealed words that were like
a song, a poem of making. *These are the words that Nineveh read
one hundred and eleven years ago. These are the words that broke
the worlds when she failed to do what the spell asked of her.* She

could not forget the Queen's failure. If Nat failed, she would damn everyone. The spell had the power to do as much good as bad. She would decide what happened next. Her actions would make or break the world and everyone in it.

She breathed calmly. *I will not fail or falter.*

Line followed line, word after word.

Time passed, but she did not sense it.

She knew that somewhere a battle raged. Her friends were out there, fighting to keep her safe, to make certain she accomplished this task.

Nat could not fail.

She learned every word, absorbing each as if it were a form of sustenance, a thing that would become part of her being.

She barely noticed when the machine stopped spinning.

There were no more lines.

The slot machine's dials were empty.

The spell was a part of Nat. She knew it through and through.

Before she could speak, a vision came to her. She saw old Vallonis, a city floating upon a sea. Atlantis. She heard the words that forged the city. The magic was strong. It was baked into every brick and every bit of mortar. But Atlantis failed, and the world of magic slept.

It awakened once more in Avalon. The Queen said the words, and Avalon sprouted from the primeval forest. But the city did not last. When it failed, the palimpsest lay hidden for centuries, till Nineveh found it and spoke the spell that wrecked the world.

Now the scroll had materialized again. It was within her. She would make a new world. Nat would erase the damage done. It was time.

She removed the charm from her throat and spoke the words written in the palimpsest. She trembled as she finished each line. There was only joy now, happiness. The long night was over; the sun would once more shine upon the earth.

The last word escaped her tongue, and Nat held her breath.

She waited, and her heart drummed.

The moment stretched.

A minute passed, then another, but nothing happened.

36

WES GRABBED AVO'S LEG AND SLAMMED him down against the concrete. The two were balanced on a platform at the top of the stairway. To Wes's left, part of the wall was missing, the stairway open to the sky. The tower door was behind him, and Nat was inside of it. Drakonflame gathered all around them. The only way out was to go through the door or over the edge.

Avo pushed back, sending Wes hurtling into the door. His head hit the heavy wood, making a terrible crack. There was a burning in his skull, a deep thudding in his ears. He felt hands wrapping around his throat. Then he couldn't breathe. Avo was on top of Wes, hands clutching his throat. Wes drove his fist into Avo's gut, and the drau let go.

"If you kill me, you'll never get through that door."

"That's okay," Avo said, backing away and standing. "We'll just wait until your girl comes out. Either way, I'll get what's inside."

The wind changed directions, throwing black smoke in

Wes's face. He lost track of Avo. Wes put his back to the door and waited, the flames advancing all around him. *I don't know how much longer I can stay here.* If he didn't tumble over the edge or fall into the flames, he'd be slow roasted by the fire. *Hurry, Nat, get it done,* he sent, hoping she could hear him.

A bullet shot past Wes's head, striking the heavy wooden door just as Avo emerged from the haze with a gun in his hand. He had found the gun. Wes groped for the weapon, taking the barrel in his hand. Now both of them were fumbling for the trigger. Changing tactics, Wes pulled the gun away and tossed it down the stairs. Bullets meant a quick death, and Avo deserved something far more terrible.

The gun rattled all the way down, striking iron and concrete.

"No more weapons, just you and me," Wes snarled, ripping free from Avo's hold. "Just how you like it."

For a moment, the two faced each other briefly, fists raised, as if in a boxing match.

Then it began in earnest.

Wes took a punch to the jaw, but managed to hit Avo in the gut. The drau spit, gurgling a moan as he bent over.

Still folded in half, Avo kicked at Wes's boot, pulling his leg out from under him. Wes hit the concrete with a thud but managed to take hold of Avo's empty gun belt. He dragged the drau down to the floor beside him. He leapt on top of Avo and knocked him once more in the jaw, twice. Blood formed on Avo's lip.

The drau laughed.

Did he know his fate?

Did he care?

Before Wes could land another punch, Avo took hold of Wes's collar and rolled them both away from the door. They rolled too close to the flames and Avo's uniform caught fire, the flames slithering up his leg and back. The drau cried out as he tumbled through the flames and down a flight of stairs. Wes followed, leaping over the fire. He couldn't risk letting Avo get away. The drau would only return with more soldiers and more weapons. This had to end now.

Wes plunged through the flames into the smoke-filled stairway. He saw nothing but black, and the smoke burned his eyes, his nose. A fist grazed his arm; it was Avo, but neither of them could see through the smoke. He'd struck blindly and missed. Wes lunged at where he thought Avo was standing, pushing himself through the smoke and the black, hoping his punch would hit home. His fist hit home, but Avo struck back with a kick, throwing Wes to the floor. Avo landed on top of him, knocking Wes in the face with the backside of his hand. Wes deflected a second blow. They tumbled again, down another flight. Halfway to the next landing, Wes took control, stood up, and threw Avo against the wall. They exchanged blows in the darkness of the smoke-filled stairs.

"This is pointless," Wes cursed beneath his breath, his mouth filling up with smoke. They were both too evenly matched. There would be no victor. Not that Wes had ever thought there would be one.

"There's only one way this is going to end," said Wes, standing up.

Avo did the same, spitting out a tooth, so that when he smiled, his grin was even more frightening. With the black smoke swirling around him, he looked like a demon straight out of hell. "How's that, Wesson? With you dead like your friends?"

"You're almost right."

Avo smirked, and the flames danced at his feet. The fire made his white skin red.

A cool wind hit Wes's face. There were gaps in the wall where the drakon had torn through the steel and glass. Snowflakes drifted through the air, mixing with the smoke.

It was a long way down to the street below.

"So that's how it is, is it?" Avo asked. "You think you can end it like this?"

"It's the only way," said Wes as he grabbed Avo by the coat and threw him toward the opening in the wall. The drau resisted, but Wes pushed back, moving them both slowly toward the door. Each step lasted for hours. Avo pushed Wes backward, straining, using every drop of his strength to resist, but Wes could not be stopped. He took one step, then another. He pushed Avo toward the opening, toward a cliff higher than any mountain, toward death.

Avo thrashed when he saw what Wes was doing. His hands grabbed at the sides of the wall, hoping to hold on. He glanced left and right, trying to peer through the smoke, to find some way to escape his fate, but there was none. The two locked eyes, and Wes saw fear in Avo's. True, unbridled fear. Avo had felt Wes's strength, his determination, and it frightened the drau terribly.

This is how it ends.

There was no other way to do this.

To kill Avo, he would have to kill himself.

No time to think; no time to plan.

Nat would cast the spell. She would end all of this. All Wes had to do was make certain Avo never made it through that door. That was how he won.

Wes tightened his grip around Avo's chest, breaking his hold on the wall, twisting the metal out of Avo's grip. The drau fought back, he cursed, he kicked, but none of it made any difference. In the end, as Wes threw them both out of the opening and into the air, Avo stopped fighting and looked down and the clouds below them.

"Damn you," he cursed, then was silent. He'd lost. He wouldn't make it to the tower and in that final moment he accepted his fate.

They tumbled through the opening; Wes's feet met nothing but air.

Together, they plunged off the Gray Tower, falling one hundred stories to the frozen ground below. The world whizzed past them, the wind screaming in their ears.

The rushing of the air was like the first gasp of a baby born into the world. This was not the end after all. Maybe it was a beginning. *This is how the world starts again.*

The ground rushed toward them, growing larger and nearer.

Wes was at peace. Nat lived and would cast the spell. He'd done what he had to do, what he was meant to do. They had all done their part and now it was time for Nat to do hers.

Avo's scream was cut short by a sickening thud.

Wes heard it before he, too, crashed to his death. When the cold and the dark took him, he was glad for the silence.

He saw a flash of white from the tower.

Go, Nat, light the world, he thought as he lay dying on the cold ground. *Set the world on fire.*

37

WES WAS DEAD. SHE HAD FELT IT.
Like a knife, it cut her, making a gash that would never heal.
She felt it in her heart. He was no more. She saw his final moments: the smoke and the sky and the earth hurtling toward
him. His pain was an echo. She felt it once, before it was gone
again. He was gone. She searched for him in the darkness, for
any trace of his being. *Are you out there still? Will you come back
to me?* The Merlin had said that there were many worlds and
many futures; she hoped in some other world they were together, that he didn't have to die so she could live, that there
was a world where they could be together.

*I don't live in that world. This one is corrupt; the graylands and
the blue are fractured.* Still, she searched for him. She rum-
maged for his spirit. How did he smell, and what shade were
his eyes? She recalled the rush of her heart when he came
close, the way his skin felt when she ran her fingers across.
They'd had so little time together—even her memories were
few and fading. *Don't go,* she wished, but she knew he was

gone. She searched but she could not find him. Even the echo had faded.

She was alone.

What do I do?

Silence.

The spell had failed.

She had failed.

Everyone was dead for nothing.

She had said the words, but the world was unchanged.

Nothing happened.

Except now the casino was gone. Nat stood in the burned-out wreckage of the Gray Tower.

In an empty room.

She lifted her chin. Through cracks in the walls, she saw the gray sky. The tang of rusted metal filled her nose. Black smoke swirled around the tower, and she saw flames at the edges of the door.

This wasn't what was supposed to happen.

Where was the new world? Had they all died for nothing?

She looked at the city beyond, searched for some sign of her magic. A clue that the world was changing. But there were only gray towers and white snow. The sky was as bland as the earth, all of it gray and lifeless. All of it ruined.

"I've failed," she said. "It's over."

She heard the flapping of wings. A black-winged creature flickered in the distance.

No, a familiar voice boomed in her thoughts. *You have not yet begun.*

Drakon Mainas circled the tower, coming closer, breathing

flame. The black-scaled beast tore through what remained of the tower's shattered walls, sending dust and snow hurtling through the air. She saw that the drakon had been here before, that it had tried to save Wes. But he couldn't be saved, she knew that now. He was never meant to live, not in this world. None of them were. The drakonfire abated and she walked to the edge of the room. Below, she saw the ground. She looked away, backing up a bit as her drakon approached.

The creature landed in the hollow it had made in the tower's core. Her steed had come to her. She was still numb from Wes's sacrifice, from her own failure to cast the spell. She felt like a ghost, as if she were watching from outside of her body. None of this seemed real.

It is time, her drakon sent.

No, no, she said. Not yet. She wasn't ready. She knew what was next and it frightened her.

Everyone you love will be destroyed.

They were all gone now.

Except Mainas.

The drakon's voice was her voice, it was in her head. She knew the words before they were spoken. *The blood of drakons forged the world. Our blood maintained Vallonis through all its incarnations. Our blood is the primal source of magic, of power.*

Take that strength.

Forge the ring.

Fulfill your destiny.

"No," she cried. "There must another way. I'll try again. I'll say the words until they stick."

There is no other path. There never was one. The blood is yours—take it.

The drakon crawled toward her and reared up on its hind legs, exposing its chest. She saw the shape of its great and powerful heart beating beneath black scales. This was the last of the drakons, the last of the great ones that forged the world.

Her task seemed impossible.

She had not thought she would need to slay her drakon.

The heart that beat beneath those scales was her own.

She pressed the tip of her sword to its flesh.

Do it! the drakon thundered in her thoughts, but the strength was gone from her limbs. The sword rested against the drakon's scales, but she could not take its life.

There must be another way. She said it over and over as the tears flowed. Of all the endings she had imagined for herself, this one had never entered her thoughts. To lose Wes and her drakon, it seemed impossible.

They stood, poised in the cold like two soldiers entrenched in some unsolvable conflict. She imagined herself plunging the blade into the drakon's heart, but the thought repulsed her. She tightened her grip on the blade, steeling herself for the task ahead. But she could not proceed. She couldn't finish it, not alone. She needed help for this last sacrifice.

There was only the drakon now, and they would need to do this as one.

"We'll do it together," she said, though she could not believe the words had escaped her lips.

Nat's fingers tightened on the shaft.

The drakon tensed. It did not want to die, though it knew

there was no other way. Even the doomed rally against the end.

Even if death is inevitable, we still fight it, she thought as they shivered once more in the cold, the weight of the moment pressing down on them, weakening them. Dark smoke wrapped them in its gray tendrils. Her hands shivered on the hilt, the cold air making them numb. She held on to the grip, and her fingers turned white. She planted her feet firmly on the floor, but she could not move. She would not budge. So the drakon made the first move. It pressed its chest to the blade and the tip pierced the soft spot between two scales. The first cut drew a narrow line of blood. She recoiled momentarily, wondering whether she could do this, whether she could kill a part of herself. The creature waited for Nat to deal the deathblow, but she wouldn't budge. Every fiber of her being cried out to her, telling her to stop, to halt what she was doing. It was just too terrible.

How will I do this?

I will help you, came the drakon's voice. It was the last time it spoke to her. Neither had the strength to do it alone, so they did it together.

Little by little, inch by inch, Nat advanced.

The rending of the flesh was almost too much to bear.

End this! something cried within her.

I would sacrifice all, I would give everything, she had said to the Merlin.

And so, with a great scream, she plunged her sword deep into the drakon's hide, deep into its cold heart of dread. And the sound of the drakon's last cry was the sound of the world shattering. It was the last whimper of the old magic as it left the world.

Mainas didn't slump to the ground. The drakon was no common animal. It would not molder in the gray tower; the worms would not touch its carcass. The drakon would end as it began. It was born in fire and it would die in it.

The drakon exploded, filling the air with flame, turning into dust and diamond, and when she removed her arm, she was holding not her sword but two rings.

The ring of Avalon.

The ring of Atlantis.

Covered in the fire and blood of the drakon, she willed a new ring into being, forging one from two, creating something from nothing, shaping the ether.

When it was done, she wore only one ring, twined in silver and gold, twisted into a new shape, for a new world.

She raised the ring to the light and caught her reflection in a mirror that appeared out of the ether.

Avalon's Mirror.

And inside it, she saw a Queen.

38

THE QUEEN WORE A STAR-BRIGHT coronet on her brow, and robes of starshine and moonlight. Her hair was dark as the skies and her eyes as green as soft summer grass. She was the Queen of Avalon.

She looked into Avalon's Mirror and the mists parted to show her what she needed to see: the future as only she could shape it, the various roads ahead, the consequences of every decision.

She saw great armies in battle, shining cities laid to ruin, smoking and destroyed. Blood spilled on a great tundra of white. Bodies piled in stacks, burning.

The whole world on fire, hope lost, civilization a memory.

Every path, every possibility, led to devastation, to the end of everything.

The end of the world.

Every path, save for one.

The only way forward to a new beginning led to a golden ring within a gray tower.

But if she chose that path, that future, everyone she loved would die.

No one would survive.

Not even her.

She studied the mirror at length, then stepped away, closing her eyes. Things were what they were. Avalon could not save the future from itself.

Only one person could do that, she knew.

And in that moment, everything was decided.

She chose the path. The one that doomed them all, that led to all their deaths.

Nat said the words again, the words of the spell, the words of making . . .

The spell was cast. The path decided. Nat lived it all again. Waking up in a prison cell at MacArthur Med. Falling fifty feet from the sky. Hiding in New Vegas. Meeting Wes. The journey across the toxic ocean. The faces of her friends. Faix. Vallonis. Nineveh. Merlin.

Wes. Wes. Wes.

Dead on the cold ground.

She sacrificed them all, gave everything to the task of creation.

The spell consumed their lives.

The world was bathed in drakonfire.

AFTER

THE NEW WORLD

THE CROWD THAT WAS HEADED FOR the wedding chapel was certainly a merry one, Nat thought, marveling at the golden sylph in the brilliant white dress leaning on the handsome soldier with the neat goatee. She'd seen many weddings during her time at the Wingate, but this one looked special. There was a glow and a joy to the group that was infectious; even the two smallmen held sparklers. She envied their camaraderie, the easy way they had with one another.

She collected the chips from the last round, bantering with Manny, who was pit boss tonight.

It was hot in the desert, but cool inside the casino.

As Nat laid down the cards, two silver chips were placed on the green felt. She looked up to meet a pair of warm brown eyes. One of the soldiers from the wedding party—the painfully handsome one with the dark messy hair that fell over his dark eyes and the sexy grin. She'd noticed him from across the room, feeling her skin tingle when he caught her looking.

"Platinum chips." She whistled. "That's almost fifty large. Are you sure?"

"Positive."

The young boy next to him, skinny and energetic, laughed. "If you lose it all tonight, don't come asking me for credit."

"Come on, Farouk, join me, we'll all get rich together."

"Fine," the kid said, digging in his pocket for a chip or two.

Now the whole party was crowded around the table. The smallmen jostled for space, while the bride and groom watched with amused expressions. Nat noted the magician corps ring the bride wore on her right hand.

"What unit?" she asked.

"Winged cavalry," the girl said.

"I'm thinking of joining up," Nat told her. "I have a mount that could be useful."

"Do it," the bride said. "Although if you're looking for action, there isn't much. Mostly, it's a chance to see the world." It was a peaceful time.

"We can't be late, we have the next Elvis," said the groom, checking his watch worriedly.

"We won't be, Shakes," said the groom's handsome friend. "This will only take a sec."

"Where are you guys from?" Nat asked, as she dealt the cards around the table.

"Nauckland," replied one of the smallmen. "We're thinking of opening a restaurant in town."

"So we say, but really we're here for the shows," his partner smiled, placing a chip on the open spot. "I'm Brendon, by the way, and this is Roark."

"Pleased to meet you," she told them.

"There you are! I thought I'd lost you guys!" said a brown-haired girl in a pink bridesmaid dress. She had a magician corps ring on her hand, too. She stood next to the handsome soldier, and Nat felt a pang.

"Someone here wanted to place a bet," said the soldier they called Shakes, needling the handsome one.

"Come on, sis, you in such a hurry to catch the bouquet?" the handsome one asked.

Sis? Oh. She was his sister. Nat could see the resemblance now. Twins, it looked like. Good-looking twins.

Nat flipped his first card. Ace. Then she flipped the dealer's. Queen.

"Appropriate," he murmured under his breath.

"Double down?" she asked.

"Why not," said Handsome. So cocky. But she liked it. It made her laugh.

"Anyone else?"

They all shook their heads.

She flipped her card. Queen. Then flipped his. Another queen.

Blackjack.

"The girls were kind to you tonight," she said.

"Told you I was lucky, now I can pay for the party," he said, flushed from the win.

She pushed his pile of chips and their fingers brushed. The moment his skin touched hers, she felt a spark. She looked up at him, confused, but he only smiled at her.

A flood of memories. Another life. One in which the world was covered in ice and hope hung by a thread. One in which she had been hunted and used, until she had found her true destiny and had liberated the world from the darkness and cold with the fire within her soul. She saw herself in the mirror, making the sacrifice.

She had given everything. All her love. All her friends. Her drakon. Herself.

"Wes?" she said, not knowing how it was true. Was this real? Were they really here? Alive? Laughing? How could this be?

"Nat," he said. "I was wondering when you would remember. It took us a while . . . all of us . . . but once we met . . . we remembered everything."

"I thought we didn't have a future," she whispered. "I saw you die. I saw everyone die," she said, thinking of the life she had seen in the mirror, the life they had lived in a different place, a different time.

There are other worlds than these, a wise man had once told her. What was his name again?

"Because you sacrificed us all, the world was born anew. And this time, the magic held," he said.

She turned to their friends, hugging and kissing each of them in turn. "Eliza?" she asked doubtfully.

"Beth. Don't call me that. It makes me feel odd." Wes's sister shuddered.

Wes shot her a glance. "Some of us remember less than others. Come on, we've got a wedding to catch."

They watched their friends pledge their lives to each other.

Nat leaned on his shoulder, overwhelmed by happiness.

Wes whispered in her ear, making her tingle all over again. "We have our whole lives ahead of us now. Not just one night, but many . . ."

She lifted her chin and he leaned down. When their lips met, their kiss contained the knowledge that it was only the first of many kisses to come.

"Where's that drakon of yours, by the way?" he asked, when they pulled away as the smallmen began to cough pointedly. "I heard they keep them in the stables outside the desert."

"We can visit after," she said. Mainas was well. Sleeping like a cat. Getting fat. The usual. Drakons. There were so many now. Herds of them.

Elvis sang "Love Me Tender," Shakes dipped Liannan low, and the group showered the happy couple with confetti and rice. Beth made illusions dance in the air.

"We're next," Wes promised.

Nat smiled up at her love. "Want to make a bet?"

But for once, she didn't care who won, for she already had.

ACKNOWLEDGMENTS

Many heartfelt thanks to the amazing team at Penguin who have been behind Nat & Wes from the beginning, especially our amazing publisher and editor, Jennifer Besser; tireless publicist, Elyse Marshall; and awesome copy editor, Anne Heausler. We love you guys! Thanks for joining us on this journey to the Blue and back again. Thank you to Richard Abate and Rachel Kim at 3Arts for all the support and free therapy. Thanks to our daughter, who had many questions and suggestions throughout the project. Thank you to our wonderful fans—we love our family of iceholes. ☺

TURN THE PAGE FOR A PREVIEW
OF THE THRILLING FIRST BOOK...

HEART *of* **DREAD**, BOOK ONE: FROZEN

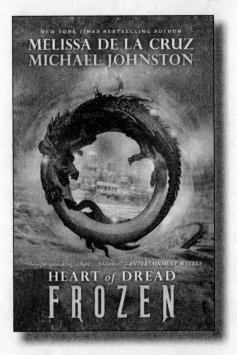

"Ice cold hotness."—MTV.com

"Everything I love in a book . . . Humor, suspense, twists,
and above all, originality. Highly recommended."
—James Dashner, *New York Times* bestselling author
of *Maze Runner*

"As fearless as a futuristic *Game of Thrones*—
and equally addictive."
—Margaret Stohl, *New York Times* bestselling co-author of
the Beautiful Creatures series

THE VOICE OF
THE MONSTER

*THEY WERE COMING FOR HER. SHE COULD
hear their heavy footsteps echoing in the concrete hallway. In a
way, the sound was a relief. For days upon days she had been
left in the room, alone, in total silence, with little food and water,
the weight of solitude becoming ever more oppressive, the silence a
heaviness that she could not shake, punishment for refusing to do as
she was told, punishment for being what she was.*

*She had forgotten how many days, how many months, she had
been left here, alone with only her thoughts for company.*

But not quite alone.

I warned you about waiting, rumbled the voice in her head.
*The voice that she heard in her dreams, whose words echoed like
thunder, thunder and ash, smoke and flame. When it spoke, she
saw a beast through the inferno, carrying her aloft on black wings
through dark skies as it rained fire upon its enemies. The fire that
raged within her. The fire that destroyed and consumed. The fire
that would destroy and consume her if she let it.*

Her destiny. A destiny of rage and ruin.

Fire and pain.

The voice in her head was the reason her eyes were not brown or gray. Her clear tiger eyes—hazel-green with golden pupils—told the world she carried a mark on her skin, one that she kept hidden, one that was shaped like a flame and hurt like a burn, right above her heart. The reason she was imprisoned, the reason they wanted her to do as she was told.

The girl did not want to be different. She did not want to be marked. She did not want to be what the voice said she was. What the commander and the doctors believed she was. A freak. A monster.

Let me go—she had implored the first time she had been brought to this place—I'm not what you think I am. She had insisted they were wrong about her from the beginning of her captivity.

What is your talent? *they had demanded.* Show us.

I have none, *she had told them.* I have no ability. I can do nothing. Let me go. You're wrong. Let me go.

She never told them about the voice in her head.

But they found ways to use her anyway.

Now they were coming, their heavy footsteps plodding against the stone. They would make her do what they wanted, and she would not be able to refuse. It was always this way. She resisted at first, they punished her for it, and finally she gave in.

Unless . . .

Unless she listened to the voice.

When it spoke to her, it always said the same thing: I have been searching for you, but now it is you who must find me. The time has come for us to be one. The map has been found. Leave this place. Journey to the Blue.

Like others she had heard the legends of a secret doorway in the middle of the ruined Pacific that led to a place where the air was warm and the water was turquoise. But the way was impossible—the dark oceans treacherous, and many had perished attempting to find it.

But perhaps there was hope. Perhaps she would find a way to do what it sought.

Out there.

In New Vegas.

Outside her window, far away, she could see the glittering lights of the city shining through the gray. Before the ice, night skies were supposedly black and infinite, dotted with stars that shone as sharp as diamonds against velvet. Looking up into that dark expanse you could imagine traveling to distant lands, experiencing the vastness of the universe, and understanding your own small part in it. But now the sky was glassy and opaque at night, a reflection of the bright white snow that covered the ground and swirled in the atmosphere. Even the brightest of stars appeared only as faint, distant glimmers in the blurry firmament.

There were no more stars. There was only New Vegas, glowing, a beacon in the darkness.

The city lights stopped abruptly at a long arcing line just a few miles out. Beyond the line, beyond the border, everything was black, Garbage Country, a place where light had disappeared—a no-man's-land of terrors—and past that, the toxic sea. And somewhere, hidden in that ocean, if she believed what the voice said, she would find a way to another world.

• • •

They were closer and closer. She could hear their voices outside, arguing.

The guards were opening the door.

She didn't have much time . . .

Panic rose in her throat.

What would they ask her to do now . . . what did they want . . . the children most likely . . . always the children . . .

They were here.

The window! *the voice bellowed.* Now!

Glass smashed, broken, sharp icicles falling to the floor. The door burst open, but the girl was already on the ledge, the cold air whipping against her cheeks. She shivered in her thin pajamas, the arctic winds blowing sharp as daggers as she dangled on the knife-edge, two hundred stories in the air.

Fly!

I will hold you.

Her mark was burning like a hot ember against her skin. It had awakened, as a rush of power, electric as the sparks that lit up the sky, snaked through her limbs, and she was warm, so warm, as if she was bathed in fire. She was burning, burning, the mark above her heart pressing on her like a brand, scorching her with its heat.

Let us be one.

You are mine.

No, never! *She shook her head, but they were inside now, the commander and his men, raising their guns, training their sights on her.*

"STOP!" *The commander stared her down.* "REMAIN WHERE YOU ARE!"

GO!

She was dead either way. Fire and pain. Rage and ruin.

She turned from the room and toward the city lights, toward New Vegas, frozen city of impossible delights, a world where everything and anything could be bought and sold, the pulsing, decadent, greedy heart of the new republic. New Vegas: a place where she could hide, a place where she could find passage, out to the water, into the Blue.

The commander was screaming. He aimed and pressed the trigger.

She held her breath. There was only one way to go.

Out and down.

Up and away.

Fly! roared the monster in her head.

The girl jumped from the ledge and into the void.

PART THE FIRST

LEAVING NEW VEGAS

Am I just in Heaven or Las Vegas?

—COCTEAU TWINS, "HEAVEN OR LAS VEGAS"

1

IT WAS THE START OF THE WEEKEND, amateur night; her table was crowded with conventioneers, rich kids flashing platinum chips, a pair of soldiers on leave—honeymooners nuzzling between drinks, nervous first-timers laying down their bets with trembling fingers. Nat shuffled the cards and dealt the next hand. The name she used had come to her in a fragment from a dream she could not place, and could not remember, but it seemed to fit. She was Nat now. Familiar with numbers and cards, she had easily landed a job as a blackjack dealer at the Loss—what everyone called the Wynn since the Big Freeze. Some days she could pretend that was all she was, just another Vegas dreamer, trying to make ends meet, hoping to get lucky on a bet.

She could pretend that she had never run, that she had never stepped out of that window, although "fall" wasn't the right word; she had glided, flying through the air as if she had wings. Nat had landed hard in a snowbank, disarming the perimeter guards who had surrounded her, stealing a heat vest to keep herself warm. She followed the lights of the Strip and once she arrived in the city it was easy enough to trade in the vest for lenses to hide her eyes, allowing her to find work in the nearest casino.

New Vegas had lived up to her hopes. While the rest of the country chafed under martial law, the western frontier town was the same as it ever was—the place where the rules were often bent, and where the world came to play. Nothing kept the crowds away. Not the constant threat of violence, not the fear of the marked, not even the rumors of dark sorcery at work in the city's shadows.

Since her freedom, the voice in her head was exultant, and her dreams were growing darker. Almost every day she woke to the smell of smoke and the sound of screams. Some days, the dreams were so vivid she did not know if she was sleeping or awake. Dreams of fire and ruin, the smoldering wreckage, the air thick with smoke, the blood on the walls . . .

The sound of screams . . .

"Hit me."

Nat blinked. She had seen it so clearly. The explosion, the flashing bright-white light, the black hole in the ceiling, the bodies slumped on the floor.

But all around her, it was business as usual. The casino hummed with noise, from the blaring pop song over the stereo, the craps dealers barking numbers as they raked in die, video poker screens beeping, slot machines ringing, players impatient for their cards. The fifteen-year-old bride was the one who had asked for another. "Hit me," she said again.

"You've got sixteen, you should hold," Nat advised. "Let the house bust, dealer hits on sixteen, which I'm showing."

"You think?" she asked with a hopeful smile. The child bride and her equally young husband, both soldiers, wouldn't see anything like the main floor of a luxury casino for a long time. Tomorrow they would ship back out to their distant patrol assignments, controlling the drones that policed the country's far-flung borders, or the seekers that roamed the forbidden wastelands.

Nat nodded, flipped up the next card and showed the newlyweds . . . an eight, dealer busted, and she paid out their winnings. "Let it ride!" The bride whooped. They would keep their chips in play to see if they could double their holdings.

It was a terrible idea, but Nat couldn't dissuade them. She dealt the next round. "Good luck," she said, giving them the usual Vegas blessing before she showed them her cards. She was sighing—*Twenty-one, the house always wins, there goes their wedding bonus*—when the first bomb exploded.

One moment she was collecting chips, and the next she was thrown against the wall.

Nat blinked. Her head buzzed and her ears rang, but at least she was still in one piece. She knew to take it slow, gingerly wiggling fingers and toes to see if everything still worked, the tears in her eyes washing away the soot. Her lenses hurt, they felt stuck, heavy and itchy, but she kept them on just to be safe.

So her dream had been real after all.

"Drau bomb," she heard people mutter, people who had never seen a drau—let alone a sylph—in their lives. Ice trash. Monsters.

Nat picked herself up, trying to orient herself in the chaos of the broken casino. The explosion had blown a hole in the ceiling and pulverized the big plate-glass windows, sending incandescent shards tumbling down fifty stories to the sidewalks below.

Everyone at her blackjack table was dead. Some had died still clutching their cards, while the newlyweds were slumped together on the floor, blood pooling around their bodies. She felt sick to her stomach, remembering their happy faces.

Screams echoed over the fire alarms. But the power was still on, so pop music from overhead speakers lent a jarring, upbeat soundtrack to the casino's swift fall into chaos, as patrons stumbled about, reeling and dazed, covered in ashes and dust. Looters reached for chips while dealers and pit bosses fended them off with guns and threats. Police in riot gear arrived, moving from room to room, rounding up the rest of the survivors, looking for conspirators rather than helping victims.

Not too far from where she was standing, she heard a different sort of screaming—the sound of an animal cornered, of a person begging for his life.

MAGIC, ROMANCE, AND DANGER COLLIDE AS NAT AND WES EMBARK ON A NEW ADVENTURE THAT TAKES THEM INTO THE HEART OF THEIR FROZEN, BROKEN WORLD . . .

HEART *of* DREAD, BOOK TWO: **STOLEN**

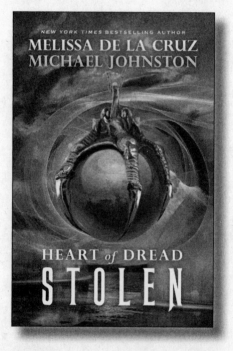

"Readers are plunged right in the middle of the action from the first page . . . an action-packed adventure."
—*Kirkus Reviews*

"Fans of the first book will no doubt be very happy with where this action-filled trilogy is headed."
—*SLJ*